I AM OSIRIS MANDARIN

BOOK ONE

NEIL BEARDEN

Osiris Mandarin Press

I am Osiris Mandarin: Book One
© 2024 by Neil Bearden
All rights reserved.

Osiris Mandarin Press
202 Oxford Hills Drive
Chapel Hill, NC 27514
USA
www.osirismandarin.com

Hardback: 979-8-9910882-1-3
Paperback: 979-8-9910882-0-6
Library of Congress Control Number: 2024916737

First Edition, July 2024

Cover design by Neil Bearden

Dear Raji, thank you for letting me be me.
— Osiris Mandarin

The reason we go to poetry is not for wisdom, but for the dismantling of wisdom

— JACQUES LACAN

THE STRUCTURE

PREFACE

An ideology is a commitment to believe what you know is false—a dark pact with fiction. These allegiances shape the world, bending reality to fit a narrative. The performance of deceit is intricate, with every word and action sustaining the illusion. Its true power lies in making you the puppet, even as you see through the deception.

1

THE QUILL

I FOUND the notebook an hour ago while tidying up after closing. It was on a table in a booth, open to a page where my story begins. Old burns from my fallen ashes gave the paper a distinctive finish. I hadn't held Conor's notebook in fifteen years. I thought The Regime had confiscated it.

Now, here it is—his words, his poetry. A voice resurrected from the past. His anger, his pain soaked into the page. I sit at the bar, a pint of Guinness by my side, smoke from my cigarette curling upwards, reading the lines of a poem I know by heart. It's the same one he read the night The Regime killed his brother.

I read it again and again, feeling the intense emotion that filled the room that night. Conor, wild-eyed with grief and fury, stood in this pub, each word a sharpened blade. His voice cracked, the agony clear in every syllable. He shouted, I will burn down the whole goddamn world.

Tears well up in my eyes, blurring the words on the page.

I wipe them away with the back of my hand, taking another drag on my cigarette. The memories flood back: Maureen, my wife, relentless in her resistance, writing about Conor and his brother. Her determination, her defiance. And then Mary, our sweet little Mary, blown up in a Renault. Just five years old. My heart aches with the weight of it all.

I can't even remember her face anymore, just her name: Mary. Something is wrong. I am incomplete. Only one thing will complete me.

I close the notebook, feeling its weight in my hands. Darkness wraps around me, the kind that never truly leaves. This world is full of pain and deceit, and I've endured its trials for too long. But tonight, the shadows are deeper, the silence heavier. The smoke from my cigarette lingers, a ghostly reminder of all I've lost.

The door creaks open, and a man enters, shedding raindrops from his coat. He moves with the precision of a soldier, each step deliberate and silent. His eyes, sharp and vigilant, take in the room before settling on me and the notebook. He takes a seat at the bar.

I was sure I'd locked the door. The sight of him, an intruder in the sanctity of my solitude, sets my nerves on edge. There is a cold efficiency about him, a predator's gaze. A man like him isn't here for a pint or a chat.

I don't say a word. Neither does he. We sit at the bar, me behind it on a stool near the register, him across from me. He reaches over and takes the notebook, flipping through the pages. He stops and begins to read a poem to himself. It's a cryptic piece about a mathematician who saw truth in lies and was driven into madness.

His eyes grow distant, as if he's transported to another place in his mind. He whispers to himself, Jonathan was right. Perhaps we're all mad.

I glance at him, puzzled, but remain silent. The name lingers in the air, heavy with unspoken meaning. The mystery of Jonathan and the mad mathematician adds another layer to the enigma of Conor's writings and our shared struggle.

He reaches into his coat, pulling out a worn copy of a book titled Echoes of the Flame by Osiris Mandarin. He slides it across the bar. When I read the first poem, my confusion deepens. It's Conor's poem. Who is Osiris Mandarin?

He explains in measured tones that Conor's poems have been published in Germany and are revered in underground circles. The poems in the book were taken from this very notebook, which has been kept safe in Berlin.

This man knows my past. He knows about the bombing.

He tells me the poems were published under the name Osiris Mandarin, a pseudonym used by various authors to protect their identities. Osiris Mandarin isn't a single person but a collective voice of resistance. By using the name, they keep the spirit of rebellion alive, a symbol of defiance against The Regime. Conor's words live on, inspiring others to fight back, to remember, to resist.

This man isn't just another lost soul in the fight. He is here with a purpose. His eyes lock onto mine, and a silent understanding passes between us. The weight of his presence settles over me, heavy and suffocating. But beneath it, a spark ignites. The anger I've kept buried for so long starts to surface. I take a deep drag on my cigarette, the smoke filling my lungs and clearing my mind.

I can't let him see my turmoil. I play dumb. I need to understand what he wants and who he is. So I nod, acting casual.

He stands up and straightens his coat. When you're ready, go to The Kraken in Berlin. It's a tattoo studio. Ask for Viktor. Bring the notebook. It's a passport in this world. Without another word, he turns and walks toward the door. The rain swallows him up, leaving me alone in the pub with the notebook and the book of poems before me. The smoke from my cigarette slowly dissipates, merging with the shadows around me.

I reach for the bottle of whiskey under the bar and pour myself a generous glass. The liquid burns as it goes down, providing temporary solace. I think about what he said— The Kraken, Viktor, Berlin. The words swirl in my mind, mingling with the smoke and the alcohol.

He had asked earlier, What would you do to get back at The Regime for blowing up Mary in that Renault? I hadn't answered then. But now, as I look at the notebook, the answer is clear. I would burn down the whole goddamn thing.

Tomorrow, I will book a flight.

2

CAMBRIDGE

My OFFICE, cluttered with chalkboards and manuscripts, carries the scent of stale coffee and countless smoked cigarettes. Every surface is covered with pages stained like inkblots from a troubled mind and scarred by fallen ashes— marks of sleepless nights and a manic quest for certainty. Proper mathematics, I believe, cannot be done without the assistance of cigarettes and coffee. I am living proof.

I move through these halls, unseen and unheard. Gödel's incompleteness theorems echo in my mind. Knowledge can break you. Days blur into nights. Equations become riddles, truths twist into lies. Lectures are missed. They whisper behind my back, their voices like rustling leaves. The Regime's influence is everywhere, even in the hallowed halls of academia. Informers and secret police ensure no one is truly free.

Eleanor watches from the doorway, with Sophie clinging

to her leg. I hunch over my desk, scribbling equations like a drowning man grasping at straws. I don't notice them. Come on, Sophie. Daddy's busy, Eleanor whispers, her voice tinged with both frustration and sadness.

Days turn into weeks. Gödel's theorems destabilize my thoughts, systematically fracturing the order in my mind. Nights blend into days. Equations become nightmares, truths become ghosts that haunt me. More lectures are missed. They whisper behind my back, concern tightening around my neck.

Eleanor sits at the kitchen table, sipping tea, her eyes fixed on the clock. It's past midnight. She knows where I am —in my study, my prison. The door is locked to everyone, even her. She hears my low, unintelligible muttering. She sighs, her fingers tracing the rim of her cup. Sophie, now five, asks, Why doesn't Daddy play with me anymore? Eleanor has no answers.

One evening, an old volume of poetry appears among the dusty texts in my study. Shadows of Existence. I don't recall buying it or remember where it came from. The words strike me, giving my mind warmth it hasn't felt in months. Mathematics has failed me, but poetry calls. Osiris Mandarin, rebirth and afterlife. I write feverishly, my study transforming into a frantic space of scattered verses and confessions. Yet the book's sudden appearance nags at me, a whisper of paranoia creeping into my thoughts.

I start leaving poems on chalkboards in the hallways, fearful of being discovered but compelled to share the revelation. They are existential ideas laced with mathematical symbols. Students pass by, puzzled, some intrigued. I watch from the shadows, heart pounding, wondering if anyone understands. Wittgenstein would understand. Perhaps only him.

Wittgenstein once walked these halls, his presence still felt in the corners. His truth tables, a method to map the world, now feel like a distant memory. The limits of my language mean the limits of my world, he wrote. My language, my world, now reduced to symbols and theorems that refuse to align. The truth tables in my mind splinter, rows and columns breaking apart like shattered wood under pressure.

Eleanor's concern grows. My office is a landscape of scattered papers and books. Poems fill the space, walls covered in scrawls. Eleanor tries to reach me, her words fading into my ether. Sophie's questions go unanswered. I am a ghost in my own home.

Richard Hall, a physicist and colleague, has an office two doors down, a sanctuary of meticulous arrangement. Instruments and equations perfectly align, reflecting his disciplined mind. He admires my brilliance but is wary of my obsession. Some minds crack under the weight of their own intellect. He has been involved with the underground network, ensuring our resistance literature reaches those in need.

One evening, Richard knocks on my door. The hallway is dark and silent. Can we talk? Silence. He knocks again. I'm worried about you. We all are. No response. Richard sighs, his hand lingering on the doorknob before he turns away.

Russell and Whitehead spent years here, constructing Principia Mathematica, searching for certainty in the foundations of mathematics. I used to find solace in their meticulous work and their belief in the power of logic. Now, their equations feel like chains, binding me to a reality I can no longer trust. Russell once said, Mathematics, rightly viewed, possesses not only truth, but supreme beauty. The beauty has turned to ash.

Helen Carter, a professor of literature, deliberately crosses my path. There is intention in her actions. We have little in common, yet she feels a strange kinship with me. She recognizes signs of a mind on the edge, having faced her own bouts of obsessive creativity. Her involvement in the underground resistance is well-known, and she tries to draw me back into the fold.

One afternoon, Helen finds me in the library, a rare sight these days. I'm hunched over a book, scribbling furiously in a notebook. She approaches cautiously. What are you working on? I glance up, eyes hollow. Poetry, I mutter before returning to my writing. Helen watches me for a moment, her concern evident.

Helen, the poet, and I met at a faculty mixer. Her thoughts on existentialism intrigued me. She once shared a poem about the futility of searching for meaning. I scoffed then, but now I understand.

Eleanor met me at a university lecture. She was brilliant, intense, and captivating. Our early years were filled with fervent debates and late-night conversations. But as my obsession grew, Eleanor felt increasingly isolated. She watched helplessly as the man she loved became a stranger.

One night, Eleanor sat at the kitchen table with my notebook in front of her. She traced the erratic lines of my handwriting, trying to find some semblance of the man she married. Sophie slept upstairs, unaware of the turmoil below.

Richard stood at my door, knocking. Can we talk? Silence. I'm worried about you. We all are. No response.

Helen approached me in the library. What are you working on? Poetry, I say, not sure myself.

Why doesn't Daddy play with me anymore? Eleanor sighed. Daddy's busy, sweetheart.

Eleanor stands in the doorway, a shadow in the dim light. Please, talk to me. I don't look up. I'm close, Eleanor. So close. Close to what? Her voice cracks. Understanding, I whisper, scribbling furiously.

I think back to the early days. Eleanor, with her eyes bright with curiosity, challenging my theories. Sophie, a baby then, cradled in my arms as I read her bedtime stories. Now, I am a stranger to them, wandering through my own desolation.

Eleanor finds my note, a mix of math and poetry. She reads it aloud, voice trembling. I have transcended logic. Don't look for me.

Eleanor stands by the river, Sophie's hand in hers. They watch the water, my notebook clutched tightly. Cambridge's spires in the distance. A quiet strength emerges within her, a resolve to find meaning amidst the madness.

My search for truth led me to the brink of madness. My verses, filled with my struggle, reflect my journey. Eleanor and Sophie, left behind, find a strange solace in my words.

They stand together, facing the unknown with a quiet strength. Madness and truth intertwined, a paradox that will haunt them forever.

Eleanor suggests we get coffee at our favorite spot. We sit in the corner, shadows dancing on the walls. She sips her latte and scans my face. You look tired, she says. I nod and light a cigarette. Smoke curls around us, rising like unanswered questions. I need to send some letters, I say, avoiding her gaze. She watches me, concern etched in her features.

The post office smells of ink and paper, a refuge from my spiraling thoughts. I hand over the letters, each addressed to different parts of the world. The clerk, an older man with glasses perched on his nose, gives me a curious glance. I feel his suspicion and the judgment in his gaze. I turn away, the weight of unsent thoughts heavy in my pockets.

A sunny afternoon in the garden. Sophie plays with her dolls, her laughter like music. A wasp buzzes near her, unnoticed. Suddenly, a cry. She clutches her arm, tears streaming down her face. Eleanor rushes over, panic in her eyes. I stand frozen, watching. The wasp stings her, a sharp reminder of our fragility.

I find myself back in the library, surrounded by ancient books and forgotten knowledge. Helen sits across from me, her gaze intense. You're slipping away, she says softly. I nod, unable to meet her eyes. I found something, I whisper. A truth beyond logic. She leans in, her voice barely above a whisper. Be careful, Jonathan. Some truths can't be undone.

Eleanor confronts me in the kitchen, anger and sadness in her eyes. You're leaving us, she says, her voice trembling. I don't respond. The walls rattle when she shuts the door.

I stand by the river, the notebook in my hand. Cambridge's spires loom in the distance, a reminder of the world I am leaving behind. The water flows, carrying away my thoughts, my fears, my hopes. I take a deep breath, the weight of my decisions heavy on my shoulders.

Richard finds me in the park, sitting on a bench, staring at the horizon. He sits next to me, his presence a quiet comfort. You don't have to do this alone, he says. I shake my head. Some journeys can't be shared. He nods, understanding, yet the sadness in his eyes mirrors my own.

I sit in my study, the walls closing in. Poems, equations, fragments of a mind unraveling. I write feverishly, the words a desperate attempt to capture the truth. Osiris Mandarin. A name, a symbol, a new identity. I am reborn in the fever of my thoughts.

> Voids within voids,
> fractures unseen,
> where logic slips away,
> truths, half-formed faith,
> disintegrate, in endless recursion.

The last lines of my poem lingered in the silence, each word a step deeper into the abyss. Exhausted, I slumped back in my chair, my eyes wandering over the cluttered desk. Shadows of Existence by Osiris Mandarin lay among my scattered notes. Had it always been there? My memory wavered. A library in Berlin came to mind—had I discovered the book there, or was it a figment of my fevered imagination?

The lines blurred as fatigue overtook me, but the memory, or illusion of it, remained. The library in Berlin—if it existed—held the answers I sought. There was no doubt, perhaps.

3

THE LIBRARY

THE LIBRARY in Berlin stood as a silent guardian against The Regime's reach. During the day, it housed forgotten knowledge, overshadowed by authoritarian control. At night, it became a sanctuary for the resistance, where whispered plans and meetings took shape under shadows and cigarette smoke.

I walked the empty aisles, my mind a vault of suppressed knowledge. My life had turned into this nocturnal vigil after The Regime blacklisted me for my subversive ideas. Once a renowned linguist and scholar, I now found solace in the musty scent of old books and the rustle of pages.

I had dedicated my career to deciphering medieval texts. My expertise spanned the cryptic verses of the Voynich Manuscript to Hildegard of Bingen's esoteric writings. My work on the Codex Gigas earned international acclaim before The Regime silenced me.

As I lit another cigarette, my thoughts wandered to the

hidden notebooks of Osiris Mandarin. The poet's writings had become a symbol for the resistance. Each poem spoke to the struggle against oppression. I collected and preserved these works, convinced of their importance.

The Regime felt not recent but an ever-present shadow throughout history, always stifling dissent. Osiris Mandarin was the counterbalance, the eternal voice of resistance.

My paranoia about the manuscript's sudden appearance in the library was constant. The notebook I found one evening seemed too perfect. How could such an artifact simply appear? Was it planted? By whom? These questions gnawed at me.

One cold night, I sat in my small, dimly lit office, the cigarette smoke forming ghostly patterns. I meticulously cataloged the latest addition to my collection, a tattered notebook filled with Osiris Mandarin's dense poetry. The handwriting varied, suggesting multiple authors over different eras, yet all under the same pseudonym.

As I pored over the text, a passage caught my eye. It described a scene so vivid it had to be autobiographical. The author spoke of a smoky pub in Ireland, etched in ancient wood with the question, Who is Osiris Mandarin? This stirred a memory. Finn O'Malley's pub, The Quill, had been mentioned among the resistance. Finn, a pub owner, was writing as Osiris Mandarin, spreading messages of defiance. It was a dangerous game, one that connected us across miles and layers of secrecy.

My obsession with Osiris Mandarin grew. Each poem, each fragment of text, was a piece of a larger puzzle. I saw patterns and connections that spanned centuries. The more I read, the more I was convinced The Regime's current iteration was just the latest in a long line of oppressive powers, each countered by a new Osiris Mandarin.

One evening, I discovered a coded message within the margins of a poem. My palms began to sweat as I deciphered the text, revealing a map of resistance cells across Europe. This was not just poetry; it was a strategic manual for rebellion. The realization filled me with both hope and dread. The Regime was unforgiving, but so was the spirit of resistance.

As dawn approached, I extinguished my cigarette and locked the latest manuscripts in a hidden safe. My role was clear: preserve these writings to ensure the voice of Osiris Mandarin would not be silenced. The library, with its vast collection of books, was more than just a building; it was a fortress of defiance, a monument to the power of words.

I knew my work was dangerous. The Regime's surveillance was constant, and any misstep could lead to my discovery. But I also knew these writings held the key to understanding and perhaps overthrowing the oppressive powers.

One night, I discovered a poem tucked between the pages of an old book on the Gnostics. The poem was handwritten and signed by Osiris Mandarin. It spoke of shadows and resistance, of voices silenced yet unbroken. It was a hammer. It needed a fist.

It was not for me. But I knew where it needed to go. To a man in East Berlin, whose verses would become a guiding light for truth seekers. I carefully folded the poem, placed it in an envelope, and addressed it to him, using the secretive network that ensured our messages reached their destinations without detection.

As I sealed the envelope, a strange mix of hope and trepidation washed over me. This small act, this fragile connection between poets, was a defiant whisper against the silence imposed by The Regime. The poem was on its way, carrying the weight of our collective struggle.

The library had given me another clue, another path to follow. The man in East Berlin awaited, and with him, the next piece of the puzzle in our fight against The Regime.

The rain outside continued to fall, each drop a reminder of the world's harsh realities. But within the walls of the library, I found a sliver of hope. I was not alone in this struggle. The words of Osiris Mandarin connected me to a larger, timeless movement. And as long as I had breath, I would continue to protect these writings, these symbols of defiance and freedom.

4

LYING POET

RAIN TAPPED a steady rhythm on the window of my cramped, cluttered office in East Berlin. Each drop reminded me of The Regime's constant surveillance. My desk, buried under a heap of failed manuscripts and unpaid bills, symbolized my futile resistance. The dim light struggled to cut through the haze of cigarette smoke that filled the room, mingling with the acrid scent of fear and defiance.

I slumped at my desk, staring at the latest submission from Osiris Mandarin. His poems arrived without a return address, mysterious whispers in the dark, each a cry from a shared abyss. Opening them had become a ritual of hope and dread.

I pulled out the poems, the paper crinkling in my trembling hands. His verses were like radio signals in the night, carrying coded messages of sorrow and hope through the static. They operated on a frequency that reached deep into my soul, secret transmissions meant only for me. As I read, I felt a strange sense of connection, as if Osiris Mandarin understood the boundless depths of my hopelessness.

> In the alleyways of desolation,
> shadows dance with forgotten dreams.
> Cigarette smoke curls,
> like dying hopes
> fading into the void.
> The rain washes away the sins,
> but the stains remain,
> etched in the soul.

The words echoed my feelings of futility. Each line revealed my inner turmoil, shedding light on the darkest parts of my mind.

In a desperate bid for validation, I published the poems under my own name, setting aside moral concerns. Shallow Existence rapidly gained recognition in East Berlin's literary circles. The melancholic beauty of the poems captivated readers and critics. The Berlin Review called me a genius, a voice of a generation. Invitations to esteemed literary circles and events poured in. However, with the fame came paranoia. The scrutiny from other poets and critics became more intense.

I felt trapped by my insecurities. Each accolade reminded me that my success was built on a lie. The fear of being discovered gnawed at me, shadowed by hidden truths.

One evening, I found myself in Der Blaue Engel, a dimly lit bar on Kurfürstendamm. The air was thick with the scent of industrial decay and silent resistance. The rain tapped against the windows, a constant reminder of the city's gloom. The faded beauty of the barfly poets mirrored my internal decay. Each poet I observed seemed to reflect a different facet of my existential dread.

They embodied the remnants of aspirations, now smoke and shadows, reminding me of success's fleeting nature and dreams' inevitable decay. Their recognition of their own failures amplified my fear of being exposed as a fraud.

In the back of the bar, I saw once-great poets, now mere shadows of their former selves. Their eyes bore unspoken sorrow, their words painted unfulfilled lives, reminding me of my own path to inevitable obscurity.

The paranoia grew as I met more poets. At a dimly lit café on Friedrichstraße, I observed Greta, a poet whose words were as sharp as her wit. Her existence was a continuous critique of the world, a constant reminder of reality's unforgiving edges. Each encounter confronted my own inadequacies.

With the rain a constant companion outside, I lit a cigarette, its smoke curling around me like a shroud. Staring at the blank page before me, the words of Osiris Mandarin infiltrated the depths of my mind.

> In truth's void,
> lies find solace.
> In the night's silence,
> voices whisper secrets.

Picking up my pen, I began to write. My thoughts were dark and twisted. The words flowed effortlessly, filled with the dread and pessimism of Osiris Mandarin's work. I poured myself into the poems, creating my best writing yet, but under another name.

I published the new collection as Osiris Mandarin. The poems received even more acclaim than before. Critics praised the unfiltered emotion and stark realism, unaware of the true author. I realized I could only produce my best work under another guise, trapping myself in my own deception.

I was only free when I wrote under the name Osiris Mandarin. The pseudonym allowed me to set aside my insecurities and explore the darkest corners of my mind without the fear of judgment. However, this freedom came at a cost— the deeper I immersed myself in this alter ego, the more trapped I felt by my own lies, like a spy caught in his own web of deceit.

At poetry readings, I stayed in the background, observing. The poets' words filled the room, each syllable reminding me of the life I had abandoned. Their voices cut through the fog of my thoughts, reflecting my own internal struggle.

The walls closed in. My only refuge was Osiris Mandarin, but each poem I wrote as him pulled me deeper into a prison of my own making.

Late at night, I sat alone in my office. The rain outside poured unceasingly, a shower of doubt. I lit another cigarette, the smoke curling like tendrils of hopelessness. I began to write, the words flowing with a mix of anguish and clarity.

I knew I could never claim these words as my own. Osiris Mandarin was both my escape and my prison. The more I wrote, the more I became a ghost in my own life, trapped by my own creation.

In the final days of my descent, I stopped attending readings. I withdrew from the world, my only companions the cigarettes and the endless rain. I continued to write, each poem a fragment of my fractured soul, messages smuggled through the cracks of my own Berlin Wall.

The façade of my existence crumbled. The rain became my constant companion, a continuous reminder of the transient nature of my success. Each drop on the window marked the lies I had built my life upon.

In the quiet moments of introspection, I pondered the nature of identity and the masks we wear. Osiris Mandarin allowed me to explore the depths of my psyche without fear. Yet, the cost was my own sense of self, buried beneath layers of deception.

I began to see my life as a series of choices, each one leading me further into isolation. The accolades and recognition felt hollow, empty victories in a battle I could never truly win. The weight of my deceit became unbearable, a constant reminder of the fragility of my success.

One evening, I decided to see Jonas Bergmann's latest film, Fragments of Identity, at a small underground cinema. The theater, hidden away in a derelict building, was a refuge for those seeking truth in shadows. I took a seat in the back and lit a cigarette as the film began.

Fragments of Identity opened with disjointed scenes of a man wandering through a dystopian cityscape, grappling with multiple personas. The surreal imagery and nonlinear narrative were meant to provoke thought but felt like pretentious nonsense. Faces dissolved into static, voices overlapped with philosophical drivel, and abstract sequences failed to form a coherent message. The protagonist's journey seemed like a mockery of my own struggles. In one scene, his reflection splintered into countless pieces as a voiceover droned on about identity. I took a long drag from my cigarette, suppressing a laugh at the film's overwrought symbolism.

When the credits finally rolled, the room erupted in applause. I stayed in my seat, incredulous. Jonas's reputation as a visionary director seemed overblown, yet his work captivated others, drawing them into a collective reverie I couldn't share.

Leaving the cinema, I stepped into relentless rain. I lit another cigarette, the smoke mingling with the cold drops as I walked through the dark streets of East Berlin. The film had been a disappointment, but it also filled me with a strange sense of satisfaction. Compared to Jonas's pretentious nonsense, my work as Osiris Mandarin felt grounded and real. Despite my own deceptions, I felt a renewed sense of purpose, confident in the quality of my writing.

The final collection I wrote as Osiris Mandarin, Tearing Down Walls, was hailed as a masterpiece, a dark and disturbing exploration of the human psyche. Critics praised the depth and emotion, unaware of the sincere torment behind the words. I let Osiris Mandarin take all the glory and praise. In the shadows, I continued to write, my life embodying the paradox of freedom and imprisonment.

The rain continued to fall, a reminder of the world outside. I lit another cigarette, watching the smoke curl and fade, carrying away the remnants of my falsehoods as the walls began to collapse.

5

JONAS

THE RAIN TAPPED against the window, emphasizing The Regime's unyielding hold on time and freedom. I sat behind my desk in a dimly lit office, shadows stretching long and oppressive. I liked to see myself as a man of precision, each thought a carefully crafted piece of resistance against The Regime. Yet, I often wondered if that precision was just an illusion, masking my own insecurities. Across from me, Jonas shifted in his seat, his eyes restless, darting around the room as if searching for an escape from unseen watchers.

Jonas began to speak, his voice thin, almost a whisper. He spoke of betrayal, of an idea stolen from him, the essence of his creative self. I listened, each word sinking into the depths of my mind, trained to dissect and analyze. The narrative unfolded—a screenwriter with writer's block, saved by the anonymity of a pseudonym. Jonas's story mirrored his own life, a reflection in a distorted mirror.

Jonas's emotions were raw, unfiltered, a stormy sea beneath a calm surface. I saw the real in his eyes, breaking through the symbolic order of our language. The imaginary self, the creator, the betrayed. The symbolic order disrupted by the theft, the pseudonym a fragile shield against the regime.

His voice grew stronger as he worked himself up. Inspired by Fellini's 8½, he envisioned a screenwriter who, unable to write under his own name, adopts a pseudonym and finds success. But the twist—no one believes he is the true author. It was a story of identity and deception, of masks and the fragile line between truth and illusion.

I thought about how the regime manipulated and stole ideas for its propaganda. Jonas's betrayal wasn't just personal; it was political. His idea, taken by someone in the regime, used to shape narratives and control minds.

My thoughts drifted to the imprisoned professor I knew. He had been betrayed too, his work twisted to serve the regime. He wrote under the pseudonym Osiris Mandarin, smuggling his writings out of Angola Penitentiary. His words, fragments of resistance, spread like a quiet revolution among those who dared to oppose the regime.

In the café, my sanctuary, the rain was a constant companion. The waitress approached, her steps tentative, a book clutched to her chest. Philosophical Investigations. Wittgenstein. She spoke in hushed tones, her voice trembling with uncertainty. The language games, the philosophy of meaning. I listened, my mind weaving her words into the network of my thoughts.

She was young and brilliant but plagued by doubt. Her admiration for Wittgenstein was clear, yet so was her struggle to fully grasp his ideas. She spoke of the courage it took for Wittgenstein to question his earlier work and recognize the flaws in his own thinking. I saw the irony, the parallel to Jonas's struggle with his identity. But then, a nagging doubt crept in—was I capable of the same courage? Could I question my own beliefs with such honesty?

My sister's voice lingered in my mind. She was an acting teacher, a purist who revered Meisner and scorned Brecht. To her, Jonas was a tyrant, a dictator of the imaginary realm. I saw the parallels, the metaphors layered like the rain-soaked streets outside. Her critiques were harsh but provided a counterpoint to Jonas's revolutionary ideas. Her conservatism made Jonas seem like a madman, his sincerity constantly in question. Yet, I couldn't shake the feeling that maybe she saw through my veneer of confidence too.

Jonas's next session came quickly. He was eager, his need to unburden himself almost tangible. He recounted a drive to visit to an East German underground filmmaker. The man was a specter behind the Iron Curtain, liberated by his anonymity. Jonas envied him, feeling the chains of his inadequacy tighten. The filmmaker had found freedom in a pseudonym, in the shadows where he could create without fear.

Jonas's voice shook as he talked about his friend, the thief. They had been classmates in West Berlin during a time when the future looked promising. They had driven together to visit the underground filmmaker, who was later taken by The Regime and never seen again. On the way back, Jonas shared his idea, inspired by the filmmaker's use of pseudonyms.

I listened, finding the story a confusing blend of identity and betrayal. The imaginary self, the idealized creator, was under siege. The symbolic order, the pseudonym, acted as both shield and prison. Jonas's struggle was an existential war, a desperate fight against the encroaching darkness. I wondered if my role as his analyst was just another mask, hiding my own insecurities.

One evening, I saw Ingrid at the café. She moved with the weariness of someone who had danced with ghosts. Her deliberate grace and eyes, a mix of boredom and curiosity, scanned the room. Settling into a chair by the window, she lit a cigarette with a practiced flick of her wrist, the smoke highlighting her sorrows.

My husband, she began during our next session, only talks about share prices and the cost of milk. Day in and day out, it's the same monotonous drivel. I should have married a broke poet instead.

Her words lingered in the air, rich with irony and regret. I leaned forward slightly, intrigued. And why is that, Ingrid?

She laughed, a bitter, empty sound. At least a poet would have something interesting to say. I hope the Russians invade, you know. They're all poets, every last one of them.

Her eyes drifted to the window, the rain pattering against the glass. The smoke from her cigarette created a hazy veil, distorting the view, much like the fog of reality that separated all of us.

Do you really wish for such a thing? I asked, curious about her motivations.

She turned back to me, her gaze steady. No, Doctor. But it's a nice fantasy, isn't it? A world where people speak in verse, where conversations have depth and meaning. Instead, I'm stuck with a man who measures life in numbers.

Her words were heavy with symbolism, reflecting her discontent and longing for something more. I wondered how much of her dissatisfaction was with her husband and how much was with herself.

And what do you want, Ingrid? I asked, probing deeper.

She took a long drag of her cigarette, the smoke thickening around her. I want to feel alive, Doctor. I want to escape this mundane existence, to break free from the chains of routine.

Her words matched the sentiments of many of my patients. The masks we wear, the identities we construct—they were all part of a larger game, a game we couldn't escape. But perhaps, like Ingrid, we all longed for something more, something real.

Back at the café, my mind raced with thoughts. The waitress seemed more confident now, her interactions less hesitant. She talked about Wittgenstein's courage to denounce his earlier ideas and his ability to recognize the flaws in his own thinking. She admired his intellectual honesty. I saw a parallel to Jonas's struggle with self-doubt. But could I ever achieve such honesty myself?

Jonas's paranoia grew with each session. His narrative became darker and more disjointed. He described his efforts to gather evidence against the idea thief, his increasing obsession. I saw the mirror stage, the fragmentation of his self. Jonas's idealized self-image, the true creator, was under attack. The real seeped through the cracks, like thick oil oozing from a broken vessel, dark and uncontrollable.

My analysis remained detached and clinical. The imaginary self, the creator, was shattered. The symbolic order, the pseudonym, was a weak defense against the real. Jonas's struggle was an existential dance, a fight against overwhelming darkness. But was my detachment a strength or a weakness? Was I hiding behind theory to avoid confronting my own vulnerabilities?

One evening, as I sat in the café, I saw Ingrid speaking to a man I recognized as Viktor, another patient of mine. He had the demeanor of someone burdened by secrets. They conversed in hushed tones, their faces obscured by the smoke filling the room. An uneasy tension gripped me, and paranoia began to gnaw at my mind.

During our next session, Viktor spoke again of his past. Do you know Raskolnikov, Doctor? From Crime and Punishment.

I nodded. Of course.

Raskolnikov was a coward, Viktor said with a faint smile. He couldn't accept himself. He tried to justify his actions with grand theories, but in the end, he was just a scared little man.

His words lingered, rich with symbolism. And what about you, Viktor? Do you see yourself in Raskolnikov?

Viktor chuckled, a dry, humorless sound. No, Doctor. I am nothing like him. I am not a coward. But I do understand the allure of hiding behind grand ideas.

He paused, taking another drag of his cigarette. I was once an assassin, you know. In Norway. It was a different life, a different identity. I lived in the shadows, just like your underground filmmaker.

A wave of unease washed over me. Viktor's words were laced with implications, but they remained just that—implications. He spoke in riddles, stories full of suggestions but never confessions. Bastard.

Are you still under surveillance, Viktor? I asked, my curiosity piqued.

He nodded, a faint smile on his lips. Always. It keeps life interesting, Doctor. Without the attention, I might slide into solipsism. The surveillance reminds me I am part of something larger; my actions have consequences.

There was a certain relish in his voice, a satisfaction in the idea of being watched. It was a far cry from Jonas's paranoia. Viktor seemed to thrive on the attention, drawing strength from it.

At our next session, Jonas mentioned the Russians. All Russians are poets, he said, his voice filled with a strange mix of admiration and fear. I want my next film to be about a Russian poet who writes under a pseudonym. He uses the name Osiris Mandarin. His writings are revolutionary.

He continued, weaving a confused narrative that blurred the lines between reality and fiction. The KGB detain another man using Osiris Mandarin as a pseudonym, believing him to be the author of a poem that caused unrest in Czechoslovakia. The man confesses to a crime he didn't commit. He smiles when he is shot against a brick wall. He knows his death will stir something; the poem he did not write will bring down regimes. He is right. The poem grows in significance, inspiring students behind the Iron Curtain to protest. Protests cascade through Europe. The KGB officer who had the wrong man killed is accused of treachery. He is blamed for the dissent and sent to a Gulag where he writes poetry as Osiris Mandarin. His poems ignite unrest in the Gulag. He is found out and shot against a stone wall. Before he dies, he says it is the duty of all Russian men to be poets.

Jonas's story lingered in my mind, a tangled web of ideas and identities. I saw the connections, the threads that wove through the lives of my patients. Ingrid, with her longing for a life of poetry; Viktor with his hidden past; the waitress with her philosophical inquiries; and Jonas, struggling with his own creative identity.

One evening, as I sat in the café, I saw Viktor again, this time at the jazz club. The smoke in the room created an atmosphere of mystery, blurring the boundaries between people. The band was in full swing, with the saxophonist's notes weaving through the smoky air. The bassist, a man named Thijs, had a face etched with years of stories.

During a break, Thijs approached me, his eyes reflecting the smoke and dim lights. You know, Erik, he said, nursing his drink, sometimes I think we're all just actors in a play we didn't write. Each mask we wear adds another layer of illusion.

I nodded, intrigued by his words. Indeed, Thijs. And what if the mask becomes more real than the face beneath?

Then we've truly lost ourselves, haven't we? Just like a poet lost in his own verse.

We sat in silence for a moment, the weight of his words settling over us. Thijs began to tell another story. He spoke of a time in New York, playing in a dingy club in Harlem. There was a young saxophonist, barely out of his teens, who played with such soul it seemed like the music was the only thing keeping him alive. One night, after a particularly intense set, the saxophonist vanished, leaving his instrument behind. No one ever saw him again.

Some say he just couldn't take the pressure, Thijs said. Others think he found a better life somewhere. But I like to think he became the music. He found a way to escape a reality too harsh for him.

His story lingered in my mind, mingling with my thoughts about Jonas, Viktor, and the waitress. The masks we wear, the identities we construct—they were all part of a larger game, a game we couldn't escape. But perhaps, like the saxophonist, we could find a way to become the music, to transcend the limitations of our existence.

I left the club with a sense of clarity. The rain had stopped, leaving the streets glistening under the dim street-lights. As I walked back to my apartment, I thought about the pseudonymous language game, the paper I would write, and the name I would use—Osiris Mandarin. It was fitting, a nod to the multiplicity of identities we all carried within us.

Back in my apartment, I sat at my desk, the rain a distant memory. I opened my notebook, the blank pages waiting. I thought of Jonas, the filmmaker who found freedom in shadows. I thought of the waitress, her tentative steps towards confidence. I thought of my sister, her fierce dedication to truth in performance. Each story, each life, was a piece of the larger puzzle.

My pen moved, the words flowing. I wrote of identity, of the masks people wore. I wrote of the real, the raw, unfiltered emotion that broke through the veneer of civilized life. I wrote of the imaginary, the idealized self that struggled against the confines of reality. I wrote of the symbolic, the structures that both protected and imprisoned.

Jonas's story served as a perfect case study. His pseudonym acted both as a liberation and a trap, allowing him to create while also providing a place to hide. The concept of the idea thief and the betrayal fit seamlessly into this framework. For a brief moment, I felt a sense of clarity amidst the confusion.

The next day, my routine continued as usual: the café, the rain, the steady stream of patients. But something had shifted. The waitress, now more confident, spoke more freely. We discussed Wittgenstein, the nature of language, and the fluidity of meaning. These conversations became a bright spot in my otherwise gray days.

Jonas's sessions grew darker, burdened by the weight of his humiliation. He spoke less about the idea thief and more about his own inadequacies. I listened, tracing the contours of Jonas's psyche. The unvarnished pain was evident, the idealized creator within him shattered. The pseudonym, a fragile construct of the symbolic order, barely held back the tide of despair.

My sister visited, her presence a stark contrast to the gloom. She spoke of her students, their energy and dedication to their performances. She mentioned Meisner, the truth in the moment, and the spontaneous response to imaginary circumstances. I noticed the parallels and the stark difference between her approach and Jonas's rigid control.

Her words reminded me of the need for balance between structure and freedom.

In the quiet moments, my thoughts returned to Thijs, the musician in the jazz club. Our brief conversation had lingered, offering a small glimmer of understanding. Each mask we wear is another layer of illusion. The words stayed with me, reminding me of the fragile nature of identity. I wondered if I, too, was lost in my own verse, a poet struggling to find his way.

One evening, as I sat in the café, the waitress approached with a hesitant smile. She handed me a book, a collection of Wittgenstein's notes. I thought you might find this interesting, she said, her voice steady. I accepted the book, our hands briefly touching. There was a moment of connection, a silent acknowledgment of our shared journey.

Back in my apartment, I opened the book, the pages filled with Wittgenstein's meticulous handwriting. I read, absorbing the intricate theories and the absolute clarity of thought. The waitress's words came back to me—Wittgenstein's courage to criticize his earlier ideas, his willingness to embrace his own mistakes. I felt a kinship, a sense of shared purpose.

My journey was far from over, but I felt a sense of direction. The stories of my patients and the insights from my conversations all wove together into a complex tapestry of human experience. I saw the threads, the connections, the intricate dance of the real, the imaginary, and the symbolic.

As the rain continued to fall, I felt a sense of peace. The masks, the illusions, the fragile constructs of identity—they were all part of the human condition. My role was not just to dissect but to guide, to help my patients find their way out of the flybottle.

Jonas paused for a moment, his eyes narrowing as if piecing together a complex puzzle. He reached into his bag and pulled out a book, handing it to me.

You should read this, he said, a smile spreading across his face. It might offer some insight into your own battles.

I looked at the cover—Shadows of Existence.

6

SHERIFF

THICK WAVES of fog roll across the winding mountain road, swallowing the headlights of the approaching patrol car. I stand alone, my boots sinking into the wet gravel. The Regime's influence reaches even this remote area, casting a shadow over every part of life.

The car stops, and Sheriff Clay Hawkins steps out, cigarette smoke curling around his weathered face. Shaped by The Regime, he is a cog in its vast machinery. He offers me a ride, suspicion lurking in his eyes. I accept, knowing this is the next step in my journey.

Inside the car, silence prevails. The sheriff steals glances at me, trying to piece together who I am. I sit calmly, hands folded in my lap, eyes fixed on the dark road ahead. Propaganda posters demanding loyalty and obedience line the streets as we enter the town. They serve as reminders of The Regime's control, its influence reaching into every corner of our existence.

I'm Charles Stone.

The sheriff raises an eyebrow but says nothing, his eyes flicking back to the road. We arrive at the station, its façade dimly lit, as worn and weary as the sheriff himself. He guides me into the holding cell, the smell of stale coffee and smoke a constant companion. The Regime's emblem is subtly present, a reminder of the ever-watching eyes. The dim light casts long shadows on the cracked linoleum floor.

The cell is small and bare, with a cot in one corner and a toilet in the other. The walls hum at a frequency I recognize, but it's not the familiar 11,249 hertz from my office in Iowa. This is different—higher, sharper. 49,993 hertz. The sheriff is trying something new, but the principle remains the same: thoughts monitored, identities dissolved into static.

Days pass in a blur. The sheriff comes in periodically, his frustration growing each time he leaves. He demands to know who I am, but identity is a fluid concept, not easily pinned down by a name or a story. He slams his hand on the bars, trying to rattle me, but I remain unfazed. My mind wanders to another time, another place.

Once, in East Berlin, I found myself in a similar room, though much colder and more oppressive. The Regime interrogated me, their methods brutal and dehumanizing. As they worked, I fixated on the man's watch, its worn leather band and scratched face. I wondered about its previous owner, imagined a baker who worked at a shop with no bread.

The baker stared at his watch each day, waiting for his lunch break at 2 PM. His eyes, heavy with resignation, would flick to the timepiece as he kneaded the air, the phantom dough beneath his hands a cruel reminder of scarcity. At exactly 2 PM, he would sit in silence, dipping imagined bread into his cabbage soup, each mouthful a bitter swallow of unfulfilled dreams.

I thought of that baker while the interrogator did his work. His voice was a distant hum, his questions lost in the fog of my thoughts. The baker's shop, a place of false promises, stood as a monument to endurance. He dreamed of bread as the world around him crumbled, as the shop's sign faded, the letters peeling away like the layers of his hope.

One morning, a plump deputy named Hawkins brings me food. His pants sag, always on the verge of slipping down his protruding belly. He struggles to keep them up with one hand while holding a can of Pepsi in the other, which he uses as a spittoon. He's a redneck, the embodiment of rural decay, with a permanent dip in his lip.

He hands me the tray and glances up at me, then down at the book he's carrying. Shadows of Existence. A collection of profound, revolutionary thoughts. The book is rare, banned in many places for its subversive content. But the font on the cover catches my eye—it's different. Subtle, but there. CIA font. The paper, the print. It's all wrong.

Hawkins lingers for a moment, spitting into the Pepsi can. He leans closer, his voice a low drawl. Eli is inside. He's in Angola.

I frown, trying to make sense of his words. What do you mean, inside?

Hawkins smirks, his eyes gleaming with something sinister. Part of the resistance. They've got people everywhere. Eli is deep inside. Be careful. Not everyone is who they seem.

I study his face, looking for any sign of deception. The cryptic message, embedded in the ordinary, is indecipherable. The resistance has many faces, many layers. But how does this redneck know so much? Suspicion gnaws at me. I nod, accepting the tray and the book.

The sheriff returns later, his frustration now mixed with confusion. I've called around. There are no records of any Charles Stone at the Iowa Writers' Workshop. No history, nothing. Who are you really?

I exhale slowly, watching the smoke from my cigarette curl into the air. I am who I say I am, Sheriff. Sometimes, the most straightforward truths are the hardest to accept.

He doesn't believe me. His eyes narrow with suspicion. You expect me to believe that you're just some poetry professor? That doesn't add up.

The truth is often hidden in plain sight, Sheriff. Just because the records don't exist doesn't mean I don't. Let me tell you a story. Have you ever read Raymond Carver's Cathedral?

The sheriff shakes his head but gestures for me to continue.

Cathedral is about a blind man who sees more clearly than anyone else. A simple premise, but it cuts deep. In the story, a blind man visits a husband and wife. The husband is uneasy, skeptical. He can't understand how a blind man could truly perceive the world. The climax comes when the blind man asks the husband to draw a cathedral with him. They sit together, hands moving in unison, drawing this grand structure. The husband, for the first time, sees through the blind man's eyes, understanding a different kind of vision. It's not about sight; it's about insight.

I lean forward, holding the sheriff's gaze. You see, Sheriff, sometimes the records don't matter. Sometimes it's about seeing beyond what's right in front of you. You think you know who I am because of a lack of records, but you don't see the whole picture. You can't, not with the tools you're using.

The phone rings, its sound cutting through the thick smoke. The sheriff leaves the room, the door closing with a heavy thud behind him. I sit back, my expression inscrutable as I wait. Minutes later, he returns, his face pale, eyes wide with fear.

Without a word, he hands me a twenty-dollar bill and motions for his deputy to drive me wherever I need to go. The abruptness of it all leaves me in disbelief. Why am I being released? What has changed in those few minutes?

The deputy, equally puzzled, drives me away into the foggy night. The patrol car's taillights soon disappear into the mist, leaving the sheriff alone with the lingering weight of that fateful phone call.

As the car winds its way through the mountain roads, I stare into the darkness, my expression serene yet troubled by unanswered questions. The deputy glances at me, his eyes gleaming with a knowing look. Eli is inside, he repeats, as if testing my reaction.

I remain silent, my suspicion deepening. The mystery of my sudden freedom is as thick as the fog that envelops us.

The Regime's reach is extensive, its influence widespread. Someone within its ranks might have decided to release me, but why? Was it a mistake, a calculated move, or something else entirely? Questions churn in my mind.

The deputy finally stops the car at the edge of town. He looks at me with a mix of curiosity and confusion. I step out, the cold air biting at my skin. The journey is far from over, and the questions still linger, but I feel a sense of purpose. The Regime's shadow is long, but even the darkest night must give way to dawn.

With that thought, I begin to walk, my steps breaking the silence. The road ahead is uncertain, but I will keep moving forward, seeking the truth and challenging the roles we have been given. In the end, we are all part of the story, and every move we make matters.

The mystery of Osiris Mandarin lingers in the air, an enigma wrapped in fog, leaving me to wonder what power lay behind the sheriff's sudden change of heart and the contents of that phone call that changed everything.

7

SPARTAN

THE RAIN POUNDS against the windows of my Berlin safe
house, each drop a countdown to my next assignment. The
dim light from a solitary lamp casts long shadows across the
room, mingling with the cold silence. I sit at a battered desk,
staring at the classified dossier marked Operation Mandrake.

Officially, I don't exist. Unofficially, I'm the blade in the
dark, the whisper of death that brings nightmares to those
who threaten The Regime. Tonight, my target is Osiris
Mandarin, a name spoken in the corridors of power with a
mix of fear and respect. His writings have sparked unrest
across Europe, becoming a rallying cry for revolutionaries
and dissidents.

I open the dossier, my eyes scanning the details with
the precision of a Spartan general preparing for battle.
Osiris is an enigma, a ghost. No known photograph, no
confirmed identity. Just a pseudonym that has become a
symbol of resistance. My orders are clear: eliminate the

threat, silence the voice. There is no room for curiosity or ideals.

I pick up my Colt 1911, a reliable and precise weapon. Every day, I field-strip and clean it, a ritual that grounds me in routine and discipline. Press-checking it each time I pick it up is muscle memory, a habit ingrained in my Spartan upbringing. Always ready, always prepared.

The streets of East Berlin stretch before me like the veins of a dying animal, every turn and alley a part of its failing body. I navigate them with ease, each step part of a strategy to checkmate my adversary. The rain-soaked cobblestones gleam under the flickering streetlights, the air thick with the scent of decay and defiance. As I walk, my thoughts drift to the newspaper headlines I saw this morning: President Nixon Resigns Amid Watergate Scandal and IRA Bombing in London Kills 21.

The apartment building looms ahead, its facade crumbling, a relic of a city divided by ideology and fear. I ascend the stairs silently, my senses attuned to every creak and groan of the ancient structure. The door to the target's apartment is ajar. An invitation or a trap? I draw my 1911, the cold metal a familiar comfort in my hand.

Papers are strewn across a cluttered desk, the walls adorned with revolutionary slogans and cryptic verses. And there, sitting in the flickering candlelight, is Osiris Mandarin. His eyes are calm, almost amused. He speaks my name, but I don't respond. Words are unnecessary. I raise the pistol, aiming for his heart. Something in his gaze stops me. A depth, a sorrow, an understanding that transcends the simplistic labels of enemy and ally.

Killing him won't stop the movement. It will only fuel the fire. Spartans believe in duty, and my duty is to eliminate threats. He smiles faintly, understanding something I never will.

Footsteps echo in the hallway. Reinforcements are closing in. My decision is made. I pull the trigger, and the silenced shot sounds like a cough in the night. Osiris slumps forward, a final sigh escaping his lips.

As he falls, a small notebook slips from his hand, landing at my feet. I pick it up and flip through the pages. It's a collection of writings by Osiris Mandarin, written in many hands. I don't have time to scrutinize it. I slip the notebook into my coat pocket, a violation of my duty, a crack in my otherwise unyielding discipline.

I leave the apartment as silently as I entered, the rain washing away the traces of my presence. The mission is complete. In the world of espionage, morality is a luxury, and clarity a rare commodity.

Back in my safe house, I drink a glass of water, the pure simplicity of it aligning with my Spartan discipline. Osiris Mandarin is dead, but his words will live on, inspiring those who dare to dream of a different world. I do not dwell on his death; it was my duty. Duty above all else.

But the notebook burns in my pocket, a constant reminder of my transgression. I condemn myself for this weakness, this moment of curiosity. Spartans do not question. We follow orders. Yet, I cannot bring myself to discard it. I am troubled by my actions, haunted by the words within those pages.

I walk through a crowded market and see a young boy

being harassed by older kids. Without hesitation, I intervene, my presence alone enough to scatter the bullies. I help the boy to his feet, a firm hand guiding him up. Stand up for yourself. Never let fear rule you.

The rain continues to fall, a constant reminder of the world outside. Sparta teaches that duty is paramount, that there is no room for doubt or hesitation. The Athenians poisoned the world with their ideas of democracy and free-dom, breeding weakness and indecision. I scorn those ideals, embracing instead the clarity of purpose and the strength of resolve.

Raskolnikov was a coward. He questioned his actions and let guilt eat away at him. He was weak, unable to accept the consequences of his choices. I am not like him. I do what needs to be done. And yet, this notebook, this small act of defiance, gnaws at me. Have I become what I despise?

As I stare into the darkness, I know that my path is set. There will be more missions, more targets, more duties to fulfill. And I will be ready, always ready, to do what is neces-sary. In the end, I am a Spartan. Cold. Unfeeling. Perfect in my execution of duty. The world around me is chaotic, but within me, there is only clarity and resolve. There is no room for doubt, no space for hesitation. Only the next mission, the next target, the next duty to fulfill.

8

PARIS SMOLDERS

PARIS SMOLDERS with unrest and opportunity. I crouch in the shadows, rolling another cigarette. My fingers are filthy, my teeth stained. I smell of tobacco and failure. I've taken the name Osiris Mandarin. I light my cigarette. The revolution ignites my spirit.

With a cigarette hanging from my lips, I scribble poems on crumpled paper. My words burn and provoke. I distribute them among the students at the Sorbonne. They whisper my name—Osiris Mandarin. The air hums with defiance. Across the world, others like me fight the same battle. Our collective resistance stands against The Regime's oppressive reach.

My first poems hit the streets, scrawled in shaky, ink-smudged handwriting.

Ignite the dawn.
Burn away the darkness.

They chant my words, painting them on walls. I watch from the shadows, rolling another cigarette, paranoia gnawing at me. The fear of The Regime's spies is ever-present.

Osiris Mandarin becomes a symbol. My poems ignite minds. But I tremble. My eyes dart, fingers twitch. The duality eats at me. I'm a revolutionary poet by night, an anxious wreck by day. Like others before me, my life chronicles the struggle against The Regime's iron fist. I think of Hiroshi in Tokyo, his cybernetic work intertwined with resistance efforts, and Eleanor, whose questioning of societal norms mirrors my own internal battles.

In a dimly lit café, the air thick with cigarette smoke and despair, I sit alone, nursing a black coffee. The rumors drew me here, whispers of a gathering of like-minded souls. My eyes scan the room, settling on a figure in the corner, cloaked in shadows. He looks up, our eyes meet—a shared darkness.

Sergei Ivanov, a name whispered with reverence and fear. A disillusioned Soviet soldier, a secret poet, a man who defected seeking solace or inspiration. He moves with a weariness that mirrors my own, a deep-seated fatigue born of endless struggle and disappointment. Sergei has connections with resistance members in Berlin and Moscow, showing the global network of our fight.

He joins me without a word. We sit in silence, the weight of unspoken thoughts hanging between us. I light another cigarette, offering one to Sergei. He accepts, the flame illuminating his hollow cheeks and haunted eyes. Smoke curls around us, a veil of shared despair.

The revolution, I think, is a beast that devours its children. I fought for freedom, for change, but the chains only grew tighter. Each victory felt hollow, each loss a deeper wound. I remember my conversations with Hiroshi, who often spoke of the cost of resistance, the lives altered and the minds broken by The Regime's merciless grip.

We write to ignite minds. But what if the fire consumes us? The thought gnaws at me as I exhale, smoke curling around my face. Eleanor's voice lingers in my mind.

Art as resistance, a futile endeavor. Yet, it is all we have. In the darkest moments, it is the only light we can offer. The power of our words is fleeting. Yet, in those fleeting moments, we capture something real, something that transcends the emptiness.

Sergei's eyes bore into mine, a flicker of something—recognition, perhaps—passing between us. We are but shadows, moving through the corridors of power, our voices lost in the halls of indifference. But even shadows can leave traces. I think of the graffiti in Berlin, the murals that speak of our struggle, each one a striking depiction of our defiance.

The café grows quieter, the other patrons lost in their own worlds of cigarette smoke and existential dread. The city outside roars with the sounds of protest and repression, a screaming dialectic. We are all trapped, in a cycle of hope and despair. The revolution promises liberation but often delivers only more chains.

I inhale deeply, the smoke stinging my lungs. Why do we persist? Why do we write, why do we fight? Because it's in our nature. We are driven to resist, to push against the darkness. Even knowing it's futile, we must try. It's the essence of our humanity. Our conversation lingers, heavy with shared disillusionment. The café, dimly lit and stifling, becomes a sanctuary, a place where we can voice our darkest thoughts without fear of judgment.

As we part ways, I feel a bond with Sergei. Our paths, though different, are linked by the same struggle. I watch him vanish into the night, his figure swallowed by shadows. Alone again, I light another cigarette, the smoke curling around me like a restless ghost. The revolution rages on, but tonight, in this moment, I find a semblance of peace in knowing I'm not alone in my despair. The fight continues, and so do I, driven by the same fire that burns within us all.

Protests escalate. Regime police clash with students. I'm in the thick of it. The Makarov pistol is hidden under my jacket. Friends are arrested. I escape, barely. I retreat to my Montmartre apartment. I roll a cigarette with shaking hands.

Belief in revolution. The thought lingers. Is it worth the fight? I fought. Now I hide. Alone, I sit by the window, cigarette smoke curling around me. I reflect on Osiris Mandarin, the cost of my words. I write furiously. The line between poet and revolutionary blurs. I think of the messages Hiroshi sends from Tokyo, encrypted and filled with hope and fear, and how Eleanor's letters, smuggled from Berlin, speak of the pressure from The Regime's enforcers.

One day, I receive a copy of Echoes of a Thought, smuggled into the city through underground networks. The pages are filled with stories of resistance, tales of those who fought against The Regime's oppressive reach. The words stir something deep within me, a reminder of the power of our voices and the importance of speaking out.

A crackdown. My most powerful poem yet. I distribute it, knowing it could be my last.

Freedom is a fire.
Burn brightly.

The city erupts in protest. My heart pounds as I roll another cigarette. The streets are crowded. Thousands of voices merge into a roar. Flags wave, fists pump the air. I'm in the crowd, with a Makarov pistol hidden under my jacket. The smell of smoke and sweat is overwhelming. Regime police in riot gear form a line, shields up, batons ready.

A canister of tear gas arcs through the air, hissing as it lands. Smoke. Shrieks. The night watchman from New York grabs my arm and pulls me to safety. We hide in an alley, catching our breath. This is the essence of revolution—the desire for freedom, justice, equality. But our desires are shaped by the symbolic order. We need to break free and let the flames burn through the illusions. Look at the real bursting forth. Our actions and words are the flames that will burn down the old structures. The revolution continues, fueled by words and actions alike.

That night, I decide to take action. I slip through the streets, my heart pounding. I reach the Ministry of Justice on Rue de la Paix, the symbol of oppression. I carry gasoline in a Pepsi bottle, hidden inside a brown paper bag. The smell is sharp and intoxicating. I strike a match, the flame dancing in my eyes, and set the building ablaze.

The fire roars to life, consuming everything. I hear the sirens, the shouts. The Regime police are coming. I run, my breath ragged. They catch me in an alley, their faces twisted with anger. One has a thick mustache, another has a scar across his cheek, and their uniforms bristle with authority. I pull out the Makarov pistol and fire. One officer falls, his eyes wide with shock. The others hesitate. I escape into the night, my mind racing, my heart pounding.

I collapse in a dark corner on Rue de Rivoli, lighting a cigarette with trembling hands. The smoke fills my lungs, calming me like a gentle whisper. Every shadow looks like a threat. Every sound makes me jump. I glance around, my vision darting, sweat pouring down my face. I have become the fire, burning everything in my path, consumed by the revolution I believed in.

The city burns with our anger, our dreams consumed by the flames. But amidst the ruins, a mural by Osiris Mandarin stands tall, a symbol of our collective resistance. I light another cigarette, the smoke swirling around me. In that moment, I feel a connection to all who fight beside me, a unity that transcends the destruction. We are not just individuals; we are a movement, and through our art, we will emerge stronger.

9

LIBRUM OBSCURA

BERLIN FEELS like a stage set for a noir film, all shadows and tension. The cold air bites at my face as I step out of my small, cluttered apartment above a bookstore named Librum Obscura. This bookstore is my sanctuary, a haven for thoughts and ideas that challenge The Regime's suffocating grip.

Descending the narrow staircase, the scent of old books and dust fills my nostrils. Librum Obscura is a maze of forgotten volumes, each shelf a gateway to subversive knowledge. As I pass through the dimly lit aisles, my eyes fall on a solitary book, its cover faded and corners worn. It's one of Amnon Mint's works, a thin volume of poetry titled Eclipsed Whispers. The single copy has languished on the shelf for a year, untouched and unloved. I've considered buying it countless times, though I already have a copy at home, half-read and forgotten amid my other literary obsessions. The sight of the lonely book always tugs at me, a reminder of how voices like Mint's struggle to be heard in a world that thrives on conformity.

I reach for the book, tracing the worn edges with my fingers. Mint's words capture my own battles with identity and expression. As I contemplate purchasing it, the shop door creaks open and a man in a heavy coat steps in, bringing a gust of cold air with him.

Have you heard? he asks, his voice low but urgent. There's a hanging today. Jakob Fischer, one of the young subversives.

I replace the book on the shelf and follow the man out into the cold, the decision made for me. I must bear witness to this atrocity.

The square is already filling with people, their faces drawn and eyes averted. The Regime has set up a makeshift stage in the center, a platform of death. The gallows loom over the crowd, a stark reminder of the price of dissent.

I find a spot near the back, not wanting to draw attention to myself. The enforcers are everywhere, their eyes scanning the crowd for any sign of rebellion. I pull my coat tighter around me, trying to stave off the chill that seems to penetrate deeper than the skin.

The crowd is a sea of gray faces, each person lost in their own private turmoil. Sleepwalkers, all of them. We are cogs in The Regime's machine, ground down by the relentless pressure to conform. I see the fear in their eyes, the same fear that gnaws at my insides. But there is also a flicker of something else—defiance, perhaps, or a desperate hope that this nightmare will one day end.

A hush falls over the crowd as the enforcers drag the

condemned forward. He is a young man, barely more than a boy, his face bruised and bloodied from the beatings he has endured. His eyes are determined, even in the face of death. He is one of us, a subversive, a dreamer who dared to defy The Regime. His name is whispered among the crowd, a forbidden prayer: Jakob.

I watch as Jakob is forced up the steps of the gallows, his legs trembling but unbroken. His hands are bound, and he makes small, futile attempts to tug at his pants, trying to straighten them, to look his best in his final moments. It's a small gesture, but it hits me harder than anything else. The enforcers move with mechanical efficiency, their expressions blank, their eyes cold. They position him beneath the noose, and a hooded figure steps forward, the executioner, the bringer of death. The crowd holds its breath as the noose is slipped over Jakob's head, tightened around his neck.

The silence is broken by the voice of The Regime's spokesman, a faceless bureaucrat who reads the charges in a monotone that chills me to the bone. Jakob Fischer, you are found guilty of treason, sedition, and conspiracy against The Regime. Your punishment is death by hanging. Let this be a lesson to all who dare to defy the will of The Regime.

The words hang in the air, a grim punctuation to the horror unfolding before us. The crowd remains silent, a collective numbness settling over us. There is no room for outcry, no space for dissent. We are all too aware of the consequences. I feel a surge of anger and helplessness, a storm of emotions that I must keep hidden behind a mask of indifference.

The executioner steps back, his hand on the lever. Time

seems to slow as he pulls it, the trapdoor beneath Jakob's feet swinging open with a sickening finality. Jakob falls, the rope snapping taut, and a collective gasp ripples through the crowd. His body jerks once, twice, then hangs limp, a gruesome marionette in The Regime's puppet show.

I force myself to watch, to bear witness to this state crime. The image of Jakob's lifeless body sears itself into my mind, a permanent scar. This is the reality we live in, the brutal truth of life under The Regime. There is no room for mercy, no place for justice. Only the crushing force of oppression.

The enforcers move quickly, cutting Jakob's body down and dragging it away. The crowd begins to disperse, a slow, shuffling mass of broken spirits. I linger for a moment, my eyes fixed on the empty gallows. The square feels colder now, more desolate. The shadow of death lingers, a reminder of the cost of defiance.

As I turn to leave, I catch sight of a familiar face in the crowd. It's Amnon Mint, his eyes wide with a mix of horror and determination. He meets my gaze, and for a moment, we are connected by a shared understanding. We are all trapped in this nightmare, but we are not alone. The spark of resistance still flickers, even in the darkest of times.

I make my way back to Librum Obscura, the weight of what I have witnessed pressing down on me. The streets are a blur, the faces of passersby merging into a faceless mass of despair. I feel the familiar tug of fear and paranoia, the need for constant vigilance.

Back in the sanctuary of the bookstore, I allow myself a moment of reflection. The scent of old books and dust is a balm for my frayed nerves, reminding me there is still a place for thought and ideas in this oppressive world. I light a cigarette, the ritual slowing my shaking hands. Each drag is a small act of defiance, affirming I am still here, still fighting.

I look around Librum Obscura, my eyes settling once again on Mint's Eclipsed Whispers. Osiris Mandarin, the pseudonym that has become a symbol for our cause, comes to mind. Every poem, every fragment of text, is a weapon against our oppressors. As long as we have voices like Mint's and the spirit of Osiris Mandarin, we have hope. Taking a final drag of my cigarette, I make a silent vow to protect these voices, to keep the flame of resistance alive in the shadows of Berlin.

10

THE KRAKEN

THE KRAKEN IS MY SANCTUARY, a place where stories are inked into skin instead of paper. Tucked away in the twisting alleys of West Berlin, it's a refuge for the desperate and the wary. Inside, the air is thick with nicotine, ink, and a faint scent of despair. Here, I, Viktor, a poet and tattoo artist, find my solace.

I light a cigarette, its tip glowing like a solitary ember in the darkness. The smoke curls around me, wrapping me in its embrace. My beard, heavy with the weight of countless untold stories, hangs like the tusks of Vladimir Solov'ev. My hands, steady and precise, move with the confidence of someone who finds peace in the permanence of ink.

The walls of The Kraken are adorned with sketches, each one a fragment of my mind. The clientele is a gallery of Cold War ghosts, each haunted by paranoia, existential dread, and unspoken fears. They come to me with their stories etched in their minds, seeking solace in the permanence of my art.

A soldier sits before me, his hands trembling under the weight of secrets. His eyes dart around like a hunted animal. The hum of the tattoo machine mingles with the gravelly whisper of my voice in my mind, quoting Lacan: The unconscious is structured like a language. Your scars speak of a truth you cannot voice. Ink and skin, words and scars, all are pieces of our broken selves.

I was born in Novosibirsk, a small, grey city within the Soviet Union. Dissent was whispered behind closed doors, and fear was a constant companion. From a young age, I was drawn to art, finding solace and expression in sketching and painting. My parents, both intellectuals and quiet critics of The Regime, encouraged my talents but warned me of the dangers my art could bring.

As I grew older, I joined an underground network of dissidents who published a clandestine magazine. This group, consisting of writers, artists, and thinkers, used the magazine to voice their opposition to the oppressive government, distributing it in secret to avoid detection. My contributions were unique: intricate illustrations and tattoos that contained hidden messages and codes, art that spoke truths too dangerous to say aloud.

My talent for smuggling these hidden messages grew, and my fame within the dissident community spread. My tattoos, once merely aesthetic, became tools of resistance, each one a silent rebellion inked onto flesh. Revolutionary slogans disguised as decorative patterns and covert maps embedded within intricate designs.

One fateful night, a desperate man named Alexei

approached me. His eyes were wide with fear, his breath quick and shallow. The authorities were closing in, and he needed to get a message out. It contained crucial information that could expose a major operation by the Soviet government. I knew the risks, but my resolve was firm. We would do this.

As I designed the tattoo, Alexei spoke in hushed whispers of twisted words and monstrous truths. He was just a writer, now fearing every step he took. Words have power, and power frightens those who cannot control it. We fight because we must, because silence is a slow death.

I concealed the message within an elaborate design, helping Alexei escape detection. As I worked, the fear in his eyes slowly transformed into a glimmer of hope. This act of defiance did not go unnoticed. The authorities began to close in on me, suspecting my involvement in underground activities. Realizing my life was in imminent danger, I decided to flee. Using connections within the dissident network, I plotted my escape.

The smuggler's truck was a relic, its metal skin pocked and scarred by time, whispering of revolutions past. I climbed into the back, hiding under heaps of horse manure and strips of old newspapers filled with Soviet lies. The stench was overwhelming, a putrid mix of decay and deceit. As the truck began to move, I felt every bump and jolt, each one a reminder of the precariousness of my situation.

As the truck rumbled through the night, my mind wandered to an old Soviet film I had seen as a child, one about a man escaping from a brutal regime. The scenes played in my mind: the desperation, the relentless pursuit, the final, breathless escape. Art mirrors life, or maybe life exposes the harsh truths of art.

Each strip of newspaper felt like a layer of illusion, a shield against the truth I chased. The lies we live are like these pages—thin, fragile, easily torn apart. Yet they surround us, suffocate us.

After a journey in which I was nearly killed seven times, I crossed into West Berlin, a city divided but free from the iron grip of Soviet control. Freedom cut sharply on my tongue, tinged with the guilt of those left behind.

In West Berlin, I set up The Kraken, a tattoo shop hidden in the winding streets. The shop quickly gained a reputation not just for the quality of my tattoos, but for the atmosphere of defiance and resilience it embodied. The walls were adorned with my sketches, each one reflecting my journey and the silent battles I continued to fight.

One night, an Irishman entered The Kraken, his bright, clean-cut appearance clashing with the rough, inked regulars. He sat down, his voice lilting with an accent that spoke of green fields and distant shores.

As I prepared my tools, he watched me with a mixture of curiosity and wariness. He requested a labyrinth, with a raven at its center. The design was intricate, each line representing his journey, a symbol of his search for meaning and connection.

I worked in silence, the hum of the tattoo machine the only sound. The raven took shape amidst the labyrinth, each stroke of ink a marker of his story. The man's eyes were distant, as if seeing something far beyond the walls of the shop.

In the end, he left with more than just a tattoo. The Kraken was not merely a place for ink; it was a sanctuary for those who dared to defy the silence, a library where stories were etched into the skin.

11

PRISON

I ONCE WORKED AS A PHYSICIST, focusing on condensed matter and spin glasses. My studies revolved around frustrated, disordered systems, extracting the essence of chaos and order from mathematical theories to understand the unpredictable. Now, within the walls of Angola Penitentiary, my life mirrors the systems I once analyzed.

My cell is a cold, gray box, an impenetrable fortress. Time blurs; days bleed into each other in a cycle of eating, working, sleeping, and repeating. The Regime's surveillance is omnipresent, a lattice of watchful eyes.

Rachel, my wife, was a history professor specializing in revolutionary movements. We met in grad school at Texas A&M and co-authored a book, The Logical Structure of Revolutionary Ideologies. Our research showed how ideas could persist and change societies. Rachel is dead now, poisoned. I found her near the toilet, and the police discovered a bag of poison in my truck. The evidence was flimsy, but I argued with the judges, striving for clarity and coherence. They disliked it—an outsider making them look incompetent. I got 25 years. My lawyer said I could have avoided prison if I hadn't been so confrontational.

In Angola Penitentiary, time blurs. Wake up. Eat. Work. Sleep. Repeat. The fields are endless, the sun relentless, the guards brutal. Inmates are herded and broken like cattle. I work in the fields, my mind wandering. My interest in physics has dissipated.

Eli Brooks is my cellmate, a local who robbed a store. Intelligent but prone to poor decisions, he is essentially decent but unlucky.

We are an unlikely pair. I am introspective and methodical; Eli is impulsive and restless. Our initial interactions are terse and tense. I find Eli's constant chatter grating. He doesn't understand my need for silence and solitude. But over time, a grudging respect forms between us, born out of our shared struggle and oppressive environment.

Life in Angola is a series of mechanical motions. The guards rule with an iron fist, and we are herded from task to task. The fields are endless and back-breaking, the sun a relentless overseer. Any sign of resistance is met with swift and brutal punishment from The Regime's enforcers.

Among the inmates, one stands out. He doesn't speak much or write letters. He arrived quietly and blended in. His name is Finn O'Malley, an Irish pub owner. Somehow, he ended up in Angola. Some say he got into trouble with the wrong people.

During work hours, Finn often mutters lines that sound like fragments of poetry. Once, I heard him whisper, The sun is a cruel overseer, burning away the shadows of our former selves. He looks at me with knowing eyes, as if seeing through my exterior and sensing the writer within.

My writing is my way of holding onto my identity in a place designed by The Regime to strip it away. I write logical arguments, plain and direct, yet they feel incomplete. It isn't until I create Osiris Mandarin, a pseudonym, that I discover the power of metaphorical logic. As Osiris, I can write with a freedom I can't achieve as myself.

Eli eventually asks to read one of my stories. Reluctantly, I hand him the notebook. Eli reads in silence, his usual chatter stilled by the weight of Osiris's words.

The stories, written as Osiris Mandarin, reach the outside world through a network of allies. They are hidden in books, tucked into the folds of clothing, or even memorized and recited. Each story is a piece of truth, a shard of resistance against the oppressive system enforced by The Regime.

One of Osiris's stories, Echoes of Injustice, has a modest impact outside. It tells a tale of solidarity and defiance, of inmates finding their voices and standing up against their oppressors. The story gains traction with a small group of activists and intellectuals, fueling a quiet but growing movement against the prison-industrial complex and The Regime that supports it.

The betrayal comes from within. Eli, unaware of the consequences, tells a guard about our discussions and the writings. The authorities become suspicious, their eyes narrowing on our circle. They begin to monitor our activities more closely, watching us with hawk-like intensity.

One night, under the dim light of a single bulb, the

smoke from our cigarettes curling around us, Finn begins to speak. His voice, low and tinged with his Irish accent, commands our attention.

Jonathan once told me about Nietzsche's idea of eternal recurrence, Finn says, his eyes distant. Nietzsche imagined a demon visiting you in your loneliest moment, whispering that this life, exactly as you've lived it, will repeat endlessly. Every pain, every joy, every thought and sigh, over and over again, forever.

He pauses, taking a slow drag from his cigarette, the ember glowing like a tiny sun. Jonathan said this idea wasn't meant to be comforting. It was a test. Could you embrace this life, with all its suffering and fleeting happiness, if you knew it would never change?

Finn's voice softens. Nietzsche called it the heaviest burden: to live each moment as if it would recur for eternity, to find meaning in the constant cycle.

He looks around the circle of inmates, his gaze settling on each of us. Jonathan believed that understanding this could change you. It wasn't about accepting fate passively. It was about affirming your life so completely that you would want to live it again and again. To say yes to every moment, to love your fate—amor fati.

The room is silent. Finn continues, his voice rhythmic and almost hypnotic. Imagine a life where every choice you make and every action you take carries the weight of eternity. Would you live differently, or would the weight crush you and lead to despair?

He leans back, shadows deepening the lines on his face. Jonathan used to say that this idea of eternal recurrence was like a mirror. It showed you who you really were and forced you to confront the essence of your being.

Finn's words hang in the air, heavy and unsettling. Imagine living this again and again, gentlemen. The room remains silent, each of us lost in our own thoughts, grappling with the weight of Finn's words. The idea of living this life repeatedly is both terrifying and inescapable.

As Finn's story ends, silence coils around us like a serpent. The room's shadows deepen, and the air thickens with unseen dread. The guards' gazes sharpen, piercing through the murk, their suspicion a tangible force in the oppressive stillness.

One day, Finn is taken. The guards march him away slowly, their hands firm on his shoulders. He walks with calm resignation, as if he expected this all along. No one knows why he is being taken, only that he is now in solitary confinement.

I see it as another injustice. I know Finn is a good man. His thoughts and words are not subversive but humane. My resolve strengthens. I decide to act.

I write a letter to the governor, detailing the brutality at Angola. I include the names of those involved and the truth of the oppression. I send the letter to an underground magazine, asking them to publish it. I sign it Osiris Mandarin.

The letter becomes news and spreads, causing ripples in the outside world. The authorities at Angola are enraged. They come for me next.

I am thrown into solitary confinement, the door slamming shut behind me. The cell is cold and dark. The walls close in, but my spirit remains unbroken. I hold onto the fragments of my writing, the essence of Osiris Mandarin.

In the silence and darkness of solitary, I begin to write. The blank page stares back at me, an abyss of untapped potential. I pick up my pen, its familiar weight a small comfort in the solitude. I title my story Echoes of a Thought and begin:

In the cold, gray confines of his cell, the writer sat hunched over his small desk, the flickering light casting long shadows on the walls. He began to write, using his isolation to explore the power of words in shaping reality. His mind, once vibrant, now twisted by endless solitude and the oppressive control of The Regime, sought refuge in creating a story.

Within his story, there was a man named Jonathan, a mathematician and a member of the resistance. Confined to his home by The Regime, Jonathan started to believe that words had the power to alter reality. He documented his thoughts in a detailed journal.

Jonathan wrote about a character named Finn, an Irish pub owner who, after years of isolation due to his controversial poetry, concluded the entire world was shaped by the words people used. Finn's entries became increasingly abstract, filled with reflections on existence and the importance of speaking out. He detailed his daily life, each entry blurring the lines between reality and illusion, convinced that even the oppressive Regime was influenced by the power of words.

Finn's journal told the story of Heinrich Keller, a night watchman and former linguist who discovered manuscripts of Osiris Mandarin. As he read these manuscripts, Heinrich started to believe that he was the true creator of his world through the power of his words. His diary entries reflected his growing obsession with the idea that he controlled the narrative, that every person and event in his life was shaped by his writings. Heinrich found solace in writing about speaking out against the injustices he perceived, despite his isolation.

Heinrich's diary became an exploration of control and existence. He wrote about his encounters with various characters, each one reinforcing his belief that he was the center of the universe. The more he wrote, the more he felt detached from reality, sinking deeper into his conviction that words held ultimate power. He began to write about another character, Viktor, a philosopher who, under a pseudonym, wrote essays on the power of speech in a repressive regime. Viktor's writings urged the importance of speaking up against tyranny, insisting that silence only served to strengthen the oppressor.

Viktor's essays told the story of Marcus, a writer who used the pseudonym Osiris Mandarin to document the injustices he witnessed. Marcus filled his writings with coded messages, carefully crafted to bypass The Regime's censorship. He believed that by embedding his truths within layers of fiction, he could protest the oppression without being silenced.

Marcus wrote about Elias, who wrote about another writer, each layer adding to the intricate web of narrative and resistance. Each writer, under their pseudonyms, explored the power of speech, the need to break silence, and the courage it took to speak out against tyranny.

Jonathan read Heinrich's diary, feeling his conviction deepen. He felt a strange sense of detachment from the world outside, as if every interaction was scripted and every event predetermined. He wrote about his growing belief that he was the only real person, the author of all he perceived. Viktor's essays urged Jonathan to consider the power and responsibility of his own voice.

Finn's writings struck Jonathan deeply. The mathematician saw parallels between the abstract world of numbers and his increasingly abstract perception of reality. He started to think his confinement and The Regime's control were mere constructs of his mind, manifestations of his deepest fears and desires. Viktor's insistence on speaking out became a guiding principle, urging Jonathan to use his voice despite his doubts.

I paused, my pen hovering over the page. I reread my story, feeling the layers of narratives about the power of words intertwining. I wondered if I, too, was a character in someone else's narrative, my reality a mere illusion. The oppressive silence of my cell seemed to whisper that my isolation and The Regime's power were not external forces but creations of my own troubled mind.

In the end, I closed my notebook and stared at the walls of my cell. I realized the lines between author and character, reality and fiction, were indistinguishable. My world was a maze of my own making, each layer mirroring my inner turmoil, each story a step deeper into the understanding that words shape reality.

12

PRAGUE CASTLE

PRAGUE IS A CASTLE, its streets the twisting corridors of a court where everyone vies for unseen power. The city itself is a maze of shadows and whispers, where trust is as rare as sunlight in the dim, smoke-filled rooms. In this court of perpetual suspicion, I am merely a bookseller, a humble keeper of forbidden knowledge, navigating the treacherous halls of existence.

I am Jan, but to those who seek the truth, I am Osiris Mandarin. By day, I guide patrons through literature and philosophy, my words carefully chosen, each interaction a delicate dance. By night, my bookstore transforms into a sanctuary for the rebellious, a place where words become weapons against The Regime.

My writings are hidden within the pages of rare volumes, interwoven with the thoughts of great authors. I inscribe my messages in the margins of used books, my thoughts a silent protest against the suffocating weight of conformity. Each note is a whisper in the dark, a silent defiance.

One evening, as the city's lights began to flicker on, a man entered the bookstore. His coat was worn, his face shadowed by the brim of his hat. He moved with the cautious grace of someone accustomed to the duplicity of court life. He sought something special, a request I understood without words. I led him to a secluded corner, offering him a thick volume of Goethe. Within its pages, he found my notes, a hidden chronicle of resistance.

After closing the shop, I descended into the catacombs beneath the city. These ancient tunnels were our refuge, a place where plans were made and secrets exchanged. As I navigated the winding passages, my thoughts turned to the man I had met earlier. Who was he? What had driven him to seek out forbidden words?

In a dimly lit chamber, I met with a group of fellow dissidents. Among them was Karolina, a fiery young woman with a talent for painting. Her canvases were filled with vivid, subversive images that spoke of freedom and defiance. The urgency of our situation hung in the air like a storm about to break; the secret police were closing in, and we had already lost two of our safe houses. We needed to move quickly, for one wrong move could destroy us all.

The next day, as I opened the bookstore, I noticed a brown paper bag sitting on the counter. Inside, there were unwrapped sausages and moldy cheese, along with a note: For Osiris Mandarin. Your words have reached me. I have something important to discuss. Meet me at the Astronomical Clock at midnight.

The Astronomical Clock was a landmark, a symbol of the city's resilience. But it was also heavily watched by the secret police. This could be a trap. Yet, the urgency in the note compelled me to go.

Midnight found me standing in the shadow of the Astronomical Clock, my breath visible in the cold night air. A figure emerged from the darkness, his coat flapping in the wind. It was the man from the bookstore. He was not there to harm me but to seek help. He worked within the government and had seen things that made him sick. He needed my help to get the truth out.

Back in the bookstore, I flipped through the notebook he had given me, my mind racing. Each page was a chronicle of The Regime's cruelty, a record of suffering and resistance. The words were raw, unfiltered, a stark contrast to the polished propaganda that filled the airwaves. I reached for a pen and a scrap of paper, the need to write overpowering. I wrote about the brown paper bag, its humble contents a metaphor for our struggle.

Smoke from my cigarette curled into the air, a pale blue wisp that seemed to dance with the words. The revolution needs a poet, not a martyr. The words were a lighthouse in the storm. I had always been a soldier, but perhaps now, it was time to be something more.

That same night, Dragan visited. He burst into the back room where I was working, his voice filling the space with a torrent of ideas. He spoke of The Regime's crude propaganda, comparing it to cheap imitations of Hitchcock, but without the subtlety. It's like comparing a master painting to a child's crayon drawing, he said. This is the world we live in now, where everything is reduced to its lowest common denominator. His words illustrated the absurdity of our existence, the Kafkaesque nightmare we couldn't escape.

I took a moment to show Dragan the cover of the book I was reading. Have you read this? It's a story written in solitary confinement. Characters become aware of their existence, realizing their thoughts are influenced by the writer.

Ah, Jan, Dragan said, eyes gleaming. You are being stupid. Your interpretation is charmingly naive. The true genius is in the realization that identity is never fixed. It's like Lacan's mirror stage—our sense of self is always in flux, shaped by desire and the gaze of the Other.

So, our struggle isn't just about shaping reality with words, but also about understanding and embracing the fluidity of our own identities, I said.

Precisely, Dragan replied. This story isn't just about the power of words; it's an exploration of how our identities are in constant negotiation with the world. The characters grapple with the fluid nature of their identities.

The next day, I opened the bookstore with renewed purpose. Each customer, each book, held potential to change our struggle. A young woman entered, seeking something special. I guided her to Goethe. She found my notes in the margins, a silent exchange of defiance.

That evening, I met with Karolina and Dragan in the catacombs. Determination underpinned our every move. We had received more information from Tomas, details that could expose The Regime's atrocities. The planning was meticulous, the stakes high.

Another night, I stood in the shadow of the Astronomical

Clock. Tomas handed me another notebook, warning The Regime was planning something big. We had to act quickly.

Back in the bookstore, I wrote furiously, my pen a weapon. The words flowed, carrying the hopes and fears of a city on the brink. Smoke from my cigarette curled into the air, each wisp a silent rebellion.

Prague is a castle, a maze of deceit and power plays. I am a humble bookseller, but my words are my weapon. In this court of intrigue and betrayal, I am both chronicler and rebel. I continued to write, each word a brick in the wall of resistance, determined to remain a poet in a city that demands martyrs.

13

INFILTRATED

THE BUNKER IS dark and damp, a fitting setting for these dreamers and their lofty fantasies. A single light buzzes overhead, casting feeble shadows. Cigarette smoke thickens the air, swirling around the dim bulbs and adding to the haze. Maps and documents clutter the table where Dr. Heart stands, his fingers tracing lines and routes with obsessive precision. Finn O'Malley strides in, eyes hard with righteous anger. He lights a cigarette and takes a deep drag, the ember flaring as he inhales. They think they are freedom fighters. I see them as naive, misguided fools, playing at revolution.

Dr. Heart starts his philosophical rant about The Regime's control. He drones on about Lacan and the manipulation of the symbolic order, how The Regime twists signs and symbols to reshape the collective unconscious. Then he brings up Foucault, babbling about how controlling information means controlling the populace. The others lap it up like it's gospel. To me, it's laughable. Yet, there's a dangerous charm in his words, a twisted allure that almost makes sense.

Heart moves on to Jakob Fischer. He talks about how Jakob, a young courier, was captured while delivering critical intelligence. They hanged him to set an example. Heart romanticizes Jakob's final moments, saying he fixed his pants before they hanged him, reclaiming his humanity. He then recounts Jakob's father's revenge, shooting the executioner in front of his family and apologizing to the child before running off. The Regime caught him weeks later and shot him in the face outside a bakery with no bread. To Heart, it's a story of courage. To me, it's pointless.

Finn's eyes flicker with interest at the story. He's always admired those who take action, no matter how futile. I watch him closely, the hard lines of his face carved by years of grief and anger. He's dangerous, driven by a need for vengeance that blinds him to reality. Johny, on the other hand, listens with a soldier's detachment, always calculating, always ready for the next move. They're committed, I'll give them that. But commitment won't save them.

I take a drag from my own cigarette, the smoke curling up and mingling with the haze. I think about the notebook I took from an Osiris Mandarin I assassinated. Keeping it was a clear violation of my duty, but something about Osiris Mandarin intrigues me. It's absurd, but it tugs at something deep inside me. I've read bits of it, secretly, trying to understand the allure. The poetry, the fragmented thoughts – they hint at a deeper understanding of this struggle, something that goes beyond mere resistance. The writings remind me of those I saw in Prague, scattered within the pages of rare volumes.

The meeting drones on. They discuss plans to protect their safe houses, to spread their message further. It's all so naive. They think they can outsmart The Regime, but they have no idea the extent of its reach, its power. Heart's voice becomes background noise as I let my mind wander.

I remember the day I took down the Osiris Mandarin. It was supposed to be a routine mission, another rebel silenced. But this one was different. His eyes held a defiance I hadn't seen before, a depth that unsettled me. Killing him felt like erasing a fragment of a larger truth, one I wasn't sure I comprehended. That's why I took the notebook. I needed to know what drove him, what made him believe so strongly in something that seemed so futile.

Heart wraps up his speech with another philosophical flourish, comparing their struggle to the resistance movements in occupied Europe during World War II. The romanticized nonsense of resistance fighters standing up to overwhelming forces. The real world doesn't work like that. There are no clear choices, no simple truths. Just shades of grey and survival.

The meeting ends abruptly, plans half-formed and hope hanging in the air like the musty smell of the bunker. They are determined, I'll give them that. But determination won't save them. Their plans are flawed, their resources limited. They don't see the bigger picture, the inevitable futility of their fight.

As they disperse, I catch snippets of conversation. Finn talks about burning everything down, Johny about tactical maneuvers. They're so engrossed in their plans, their fantasies of victory. They don't notice me slipping out, blending into the shadows. I've become a part of their world, but I don't share their illusions.

Outside, the night is cold and silent. I walk through the deserted streets, my thoughts heavy. The notebook of Osiris Mandarin presses against my side. I've read it countless times, each word a puzzle piece that doesn't quite fit. It's a mix of poetry and prose, fragments of thoughts that hint at a deeper understanding. It speaks of a world beyond The Regime, of a freedom that seems impossible.

I despise their cause, but the mystery gnaws at me, a small crack in my otherwise unyielding resolve. What if there's something to it? What if, beneath all the delusions and misguided heroics, there's a truth I've missed? The thought is unsettling, a seed of doubt in my otherwise disciplined mind.

I reach my apartment, the sparse room a stark contrast to the cluttered bunker. I pull out the notebook, flipping through the pages. One passage catches my eye:

In the silence of the night,
we find our true selves.
Stripped of pretense,
we face the darkness within.
It is there, in the void,
that we find our strength.

I close the notebook, the words lingering in my mind. Strength in the void. It feels like poetic nonsense, yet it speaks to me. Maybe that's what draws me to it—the contradiction of finding strength in what seems like emptiness.

I sit on the edge of my bed, the notebook in my hands. I know I should destroy it, erase any trace of this curiosity that could be my undoing. But I can't. Not yet. There's something there, something I need to understand.

The rebels are fools; that much I'm certain of. But in their foolishness, they cling to a hope that defies logic. And maybe, just maybe, there's something to that. A sliver of truth buried beneath layers of delusion.

I lie back, the notebook resting on my chest. The night stretches out before me, dark and uncertain. I close my eyes, letting the silence envelop me. In this moment, I am torn between duty and curiosity, between cynicism and a flicker of something I can't quite name.

Tomorrow, I'll go back to being The Spartan, the loyal fist. But tonight, in the quiet of my room, I allow myself to wonder, to question, to feel the weight of the notebook and the mystery it holds.

The struggle continues, both outside and within. And as much as I despise their cause, I can't help but be drawn to it, like a moth to a flame. I know it will burn me eventually, but for now, I am content to linger in the shadows, seeking answers to questions I'm not yet ready to face.

The phone rings. I pick it up; the voice on the other end is clipped and official. There's a mission in Norway. I need to get to the fjords. Another target, another duty. I hang up, my mind already shifting to the next assignment. The notebook slips from my hand, falling to the floor as I prepare for the journey ahead.

14

FJORD

THE WIND HOWLED through the dense forest, a cold breath against my skin. The fjord loomed in the distance, its waters shimmering like a deceptive promise. This wasn't my first winter here, nor would it be my last. Solitude was my refuge, far from prying eyes and judgmental whispers. My only companions were my thoughts, my writing, and the occasional rustle of the trees.

My days followed a routine. I fished in the icy waters, my mind churning with thoughts as cold as the sea. Then, I returned to my cabin, where I wrote furiously, trying to capture the fleeting essence of my ideas.

Identity is not a fixed point
but a series of transformations.
To understand oneself
is to understand the process of becoming.

One evening, lost in my thoughts, I felt a strange unease. I stood up abruptly and walked outside, muttering to myself, eyes wild with paranoia. I needed fresh air, a moment to clear my mind. The isolation was eating away at me, the silence too oppressive.

When I returned to my cabin, I sensed something was wrong. The air felt different, charged with an unfamiliar tension. Then I saw him, standing in the shadows, his eyes cold and unfeeling. He stepped forward, a pistol aimed at me. He ordered me to sit, and I complied, taking a seat at the small table in the center of the room.

A pile of resistance literature from different parts of the world rested on the table. I was engrossed in writing a book, my thoughts scattered across loose papers and open volumes. Shadows of Existence lay open, its pages covered with scribbled notes and underlined passages. He picked it up and flipped through the pages silently, his expression impossible to read.

He finally spoke, his voice cold and mechanical. I'm Franz Keller. You know why I'm here.

I lit a cigarette, trying to steady my nerves. Solitude breeds clarity, but also a peculiar kind of madness. I had spent years dissecting the nature of identity, autonomy, resistance. Now, faced with an agent of The Regime, those ideas took on a new urgency.

We sat at the table, sipping coffee and smoking Belomorkanal cigarettes. He constantly checked his pistol, a ritualistic motion that betrayed his obsession with precision and control. This man, an enforcer of The Regime, was a product of the very system I had spent my life deconstructing.

I spoke about identity, how it's a complex and fluid concept, not static but rather a continuous process of becoming. He nodded, his mind clearly focused on his mission.

I mentioned my writings and the stir they had caused. I smiled bitterly, knowing the truth often causes fear. People fear what they don't understand. The Regime, with its iron grip, feared the ideas I propagated. Ideas of freedom, autonomy, and the inherent power of the individual to resist.

The silence between us was a tightrope, stretched with the weight of unsaid words. He picked up Shadows of Existence again, his eyes scanning the pages. He said nothing, but his interest was evident.

I invoked Crime and Punishment. Did he think Raskolnikov was justified in killing the old woman? He shook his head, calling Raskolnikov weak, for doubting himself, and ultimately failing. I argued Raskolnikov believed he was extraordinary, above the law, and justified in testing that belief. He countered Raskolnikov was a coward, unable to handle the consequences of his actions.

We debated, our words cutting through the smoke. Our conversation was more than an intellectual exercise; it was a clash of worldviews. I saw him as the embodiment of the oppressive system I had always fought against, and he saw me as a threat to the order he maintained.

I suggested we toast Dostoyevsky with a shot of vodka. He nodded. I stood and moved to a small cabinet, retrieving a bottle and two glasses. I poured the drinks, then returned to the table.

We toasted to Dostoyevsky, for illuminating the depths of

the human soul. We drank, the vodka burning its way down my throat.

I refilled our glasses and proposed a toast to identity, to the endless quest for understanding who we truly are. He raised his glass.

I leaned back, a glint in my eye, and proposed another toast to Raskolnikov, for daring to challenge the moral fabric of society. He nodded, lifting his glass. We drank, the air thick with tension and smoke.

After the toasts, he watched me closely. His gaze was unwavering, his eyes clear and unafraid. There was a moment of silence, the weight of our discussion hanging in the air. He repeated a quote from Dostoyevsky: Man is a mystery. It needs to be unraveled, and if you spend your whole life unraveling it, don't say that you've wasted time. The words hung in the air, heavy with meaning.

I looked at him, a hint of a smile playing on my lips. I spoke about the mystery of human existence, how our actions, our beliefs, our very identities are all part of the unraveling. We are constantly seeking, constantly becoming.

In one swift motion, he pulled his pistol and shot me in the face. The sound was deafening in the small cabin, the impact immediate. I fell back, lifeless, the glass slipping from my hand.

As my consciousness faded, the last thing I saw was the smoke from his pistol mingling with the cigarette smoke that still hung in the air. My quest for understanding was cut short, my life ending in a moment of brutal clarity.

15

LA LUMIÈRE CACHÉE

My CONNECTION to Osiris Mandarin started with a single, mysterious letter. It arrived on a dreary afternoon, the paper yellowed and the ink smudged. The message was brief but intriguing, hinting at a shared mission against The Regime. Captivated, I replied, and thus began our correspondence.

Each letter I wrote was an attempt to unravel the mysteries of my past and understand my place in the resistance. I recounted my days as a celebrated poet, my fall from grace, and the secret activities that had led me to this secluded corner of Fontainebleau. La Lumière Cachée, the bookstore, served as both a retreat and a cage.

Osiris Mandarin was not a person but an idea, a symbol of defiance against those who sought to silence us. Together, we aimed to forge a new reality, one word at a time. The response came swiftly, hinting at a network of dissidents scattered across the globe. My small bookstore became a hub of covert activity, a refuge for those who dared to defy The Regime.

It was here I met Marie, a young revolutionary with fire in her eyes and poetry in her soul. Marie embodied the resistance. She brought news from the front lines, stories of courage and sacrifice that fueled my writing. Together, we crafted messages of hope and rebellion, smuggling them out to the world through clandestine channels.

Marie had connections with Sergei Ivanov, the disillusioned Soviet soldier I met in Paris, and Eleanor, whose husband's transformation I had chronicled in previous letters. Their stories intertwined with ours, each thread weaving into the fabric of our collective struggle.

One night, as the rain pelted against the windows and the city's lights shimmered in the distance, Marie received a visitor. He was a shadowy figure, his face hidden by the brim of his hat. He handed her a brown paper bag, its contents heavy and ominous. Inside, she found a stack of papers and a Makarov. The papers were a manifesto, detailing plans for a major operation against The Regime. The gun was a reminder of the stakes, a symbol of the danger we faced.

We read the manifesto together, feeling the weight of our mission settle upon us. The revolution was not just a dream; it was a reality we were creating with each passing day. Marie and I redoubled our efforts, our small bookstore becoming a haven for those who sought freedom.

Our work was not without peril. The Regime's agents were everywhere, their eyes and ears ever vigilant. One evening, as we prepared to send out a batch of letters, we heard a knock at the door. Marie's face paled, her eyes wide with fear.

I shoved the letters into a hidden compartment beneath the floorboards, my heart pounding. The knock came again, more insistent this time. With a deep breath, I opened the door.

Standing there was a man in a dark trench coat, his face obscured by shadows. He held up a badge, the emblem of The Regime gleaming in the dim light.

He stepped inside, his presence cold and unfeeling. The tension in the room was thick, a silent battle of wills. I offered him a glass of wine, trying to mask my anxiety. We sat across from each other, the air heavy with unspoken accusations. He scrutinized the bookshelves, his gaze lingering on the titles. Each moment stretched into an eternity, the weight of his suspicion pressing down on me.

He asked about Osiris Mandarin, the name a dagger to my heart. I denied any knowledge, my words a fragile shield against his probing. He spoke of danger, of ideas that could topple regimes. I met his gaze, defiant yet trembling inside. The conversation was a chess game, each move fraught with peril.

He mentioned Marie, her revolutionary spirit. My pulse quickened, but I maintained my facade. The encounter was a test, a reminder of the thin line we walked. Finally, he left, the door closing behind him like a guillotine.

The days turned into weeks, and our efforts began to bear fruit. The resistance grew stronger, our network expanding as more and more people joined our cause. Each letter we sent out was a spark of hope in a world engulfed in darkness.

One sweltering afternoon, the door of the bookstore creaked open, and a man stepped inside. He was tall and gaunt, with eyes that seemed to pierce through reality. His clothes were disheveled, and he carried an air of urgency.

He inquired about Tolstoy's Gospels in Brief, his voice a peculiar mix of command and curiosity. I retrieved the book, noting the sweat trickling down his forehead and the intensity of his gaze. He spoke of truth, comparing it to the light of a distant star, its original form distorted by the journey. His words flowed from one idea to the next with dizzying speed. His eyes flicked to the Makarov I'd left on the counter, making pointed remarks about protection and violence.

He paid for the book and left, his words lingering in the air. The heat pressed down, the glass of Bordeaux I poured offering little respite. The French often complained about the heat, the government, and life itself. It was our national pastime, a way to cope with the absurdity of existence.

The bookstore became a refuge for those who sought more than just books. It was a gathering place for the disheartened, the dreamers, and the rebels. Each day brought new faces and stories, each one adding to the tapestry of resistance.

One evening, as I was closing up, a man named Philippe arrived. He was an artist, his hands stained with paint, his face perpetually lined with sweat. Philippe's art was a storm of colors and forms, a visceral critique of society's ills. He painted scenes of urban decay, human suffering, and political corruption, each piece more disturbing than the last.

Philippe had a peculiar mannerism: he constantly tapped

his fingers, as if playing an invisible piano. It betrayed his restless mind.

He sought refuge, his voice trembling with emotion. His paintings were provocative, challenging the status quo, exposing the rot at the core of society. I offered him shelter, promising to help share his art with the world.

As the days turned into weeks, the heat persisted, a constant reminder of the pressure we were under. The glass of wine became a fixture, a small comfort in a world gone mad.

One evening, as the rain began to patter softly against the windows, Philippe returned. His eyes were red-rimmed, his hands shaking. He took a seat by the window, his gaze distant.

He spoke of his childhood in Algeria, of a stolen bicycle that taught him about loss and pain. His father, a hard man, had blamed him for the theft, beating him for his perceived failure. The pain of that day lingered, fueling his art, a desperate attempt to reclaim what had been taken from him.

He left abruptly, the chair scraping against the floor. I watched him go, the rain now a steady rhythm against the glass. I reached for a pen and a scrap of paper, the need to write overpowering. I wrote about the brown paper bag, the stolen bicycle, and the pain that never fades.

A coded message arrived at dusk, directing me to the safe house at 23 Rue des Ombres. I burned the note, watching the flames consume the words. The night air was thick with anticipation as I made my way through the winding streets, each step breaking the silence.

The building at 23 Rue des Ombres was unassuming, its

facade cracked and weary. I pushed open the door, stepping into the dimly lit interior. Shadows clung to the corners, the only illumination coming from a flickering candle on a rickety table. The air was heavy with dust and the faint scent of decay.

A figure emerged from the shadows, slender and poised. Lucia Bianchi, the sculptor from Rome. Her eyes were dark, searching, and filled with a mix of suspicion and relief. She motioned for me to sit, and I took a seat opposite her, the candlelight casting eerie patterns on the walls.

She began to share her story, her voice steady but tinged with fatigue. A close call with The Regime's agents at her studio, a narrow escape. Her hands, stained with remnants of clay and paint, trembled slightly as she pulled a bundle of papers from her bag. Detailed maps, schedules, and names. Crucial information.

We needed to move quickly. Time was against us. The Regime knew she was here, and their net was closing. We pored over the documents, formulating a plan. Lucia's knowledge of The Regime's movements combined with my local contacts created a strategy that felt both daring and necessary. Her artistic eye caught details I might have missed, her observations sharp and precise.

The old printing press in the basement of La Lumière Cachée would serve as our means to duplicate the documents. From there, we could distribute them through our channels. Lucia would stay hidden until I returned, ready for whatever might come.

As I stood to leave, the weight of our mission pressed heavily upon us. A moment of silent solidarity passed between us. We were not just fighting for ourselves but for every voice silenced by The Regime.

Leaving the safe house, the night seemed darker, the air colder. Each step back to La Lumière Cachée was fraught with tension, but Lucia's determination stayed with me. Together, we would illuminate the shadows and reclaim our stolen light. The revolution was not just a dream; it was a reality we were forging with each passing day.

The next day, the door creaked open, and a man stepped inside. His face was familiar—Paris, the smoldering streets, the protests. I handed him a letter, asking him to deliver it to a contact in Berlin. He nodded, understanding the weight of the task.

As he left, I felt a connection to the network, to the resistance. The revolution had begun, and there was no turning back. We would illuminate the shadows and reclaim our stolen light. The journey was long, and the road ahead fraught with danger, but our resolve was unwavering. We were the architects of a new dawn, and nothing could stand in our way.

Just as I was about to close up for the evening, the door swung open once more. A man stepped inside, tall and broad-shouldered, with the unmistakable air of an American. His eyes were sharp, scanning the room with a mixture of curiosity and purpose. His clothes were plain, functional —a well-worn leather jacket, jeans, and sturdy boots.

He approached the counter, and I noticed his hands— strong, calloused, and used to hard work. He looked at me, then at the shelves filled with books.

Got anything by Tolstoy? he asked, his accent unmistakably Texan. Gospels in Brief, maybe?

I nodded and led him to the shelf where the book was tucked away. As he picked it up, his eyes flickered with a knowing look, as if he had found what he was searching for.

You know, he said, almost to himself, the Makarov is a good pistol. But you need to run it wet. Lots of oil. You don't want a dead man's gun, one that doesn't go bang when it's supposed to.

His words caught me off guard. How did he know about the gun? I kept my expression neutral, not letting on that his remark had unsettled me. It felt like he was talking to himself.

Heading back to Texas, he said, tucking the book under his arm. Long flight ahead. This should keep me occupied.

I nodded again, ringing up the purchase. He handed me a few wrinkled bills, his eyes never leaving mine. There was something in his gaze, a hint of understanding, maybe even a warning.

As he left, the door swinging shut behind him, an icy wave passed through me. The encounter was brief, but it left an impression. His words about the Makarov rang in my mind, a reminder of the hidden dangers and unseen connections that constantly lurked in the shadows.

I locked up the shop and stepped into the night. The road ahead was uncertain, fraught with danger and intrigue. But as long as there were words to write and battles to fight, I would keep moving forward. The revolution was not just a dream; it was our reality, and I was determined to see it through to the end.

16

KABUL

THE AIR REEKED of broken promises and mule shit. Kabul, a city of ghosts, held memories of violence at every corner. I walked through the streets, my notebook tucked into my jacket, a silent witness to the misery. The ambient noise was like cooking popcorn, endless popping and crackling. I am part of a special forces unit, here to gather intelligence and disrupt The Regime's operations. The lines between my mission and survival have blurred. The stories have become my own. I can't separate myself from the dead. I'm not sure who is writing now, whether I am a story.

David and I were on a reconnaissance mission in Qalai Qazi, a forgotten speck in the arid landscape. The village, with its crumbling mud-brick houses and narrow, dusty streets, seemed suspended in time. We were there to document the movements of The Regime's forces and support the local resistance. As the sun set, casting an eerie glow, David pointed to a girl playing amidst the rubble. She couldn't have been more than seven, her hair tied in ragged braids, her dress a faded blue that had seen better days. She was barefoot, her feet dusty and calloused. The child chased a makeshift ball, a bundle of rags tied with twine, her laughter a fleeting note of innocence in desolation. Behind her, the remnants of a wall struggled to hold itself straight, like an old man rising from a chair he sat in too long, casting long shadows in the golden light.

She's about the same age as my daughter, David said, a hint of a smile. The explosion was sudden, a burst of heat like stepping into an oven. The smell was the same. I scrambled to my feet, ears ringing, vision blurred. The air was thick with dust and smoke, and I stumbled through the wreckage, calling out for David. All that remained was a foot. Small and delicate, perfectly manicured and fresh, as if it had just come from a bath. A grotesque relic. I stared at it, unable to process the reality. It wasn't David's foot. It was the little girl's. The Regime's handiwork. I picked it up and, for reasons I can't explain, smelled it. The foot reminded me of a cardboard box. It brought to mind Tolstoy's Gospels in Brief, a book my brother sent me from home in one of those boxes. He also included a picture of his five-year-old daughter, Lucy, who we all call Lulu. She was wearing a cape and holding a sunflower as big as her head. The sunflower seemed to stand in for a missing face. Now I saw the little girl's face next to Lulu's. I asked myself, how does time work?

I placed the foot in a paper bag and slipped it into my backpack, next to Gospels in Brief. The guilt settled in, heavy and suffocating. I took David's broken camera, a symbol of our shared dreams, and laid it atop the little girl's foot.

Ahmad and I found a rare moment of peace in an abandoned building in Qalai Qazi, the suffering outside muted
for a while. We sat on the floor, backs against the crumbling
walls, sharing a small bottle of whiskey Ahmad had
managed to procure. Rumi said, the wound is the place
where the Light enters you, Ahmad recited, his eyes
reflecting the candlelight. I nodded, pulling out my notebook. And Wilfred Owen wrote, my friend, you would not
tell with such high zest to children ardent for some desperate
glory, the old Lie: Dulce et decorum est pro patria mori.
Ahmad smiled, a rare sight. We took turns scribbling lines,
words blending into a tapestry of pain and hope. Ahmad's
verses were filled with longing for a world without war, while
mine captured the stark reality of our existence.

Back in Kabul. I needed to clear my head. I left our quarters, keeping to the shadows, avoiding patrols. The city felt
like a giant, oppressive organism, breathing down my neck.
As I made my way through darkened alleys, a man stumbled
out of a darkened corner, a red beret tilted awkwardly on his
head. His eyes were wild, his steps unsteady. Infidel, he
slurred, brandishing a knife. Let's trade souls.

I found that line beautiful. I said, are you a poet? No
reply.

I raised the Glock 19. He lunged, his silhouette frozen on
the wall, like the projector had stalled during Nosferatu. I put
my round center mass, a perfect score of 10. He fell, the beret
tumbling to the ground. My first worry was whether my shot
might've woken a child. I whispered, I'm sorry.

I looked down at the man, a miniature balloon slowly
inflated and deflated in his right nostril. It made me think of

a determined child whose lungs were too weak to stretch the balloon to its full potential. I wondered whether this man had reached his full potential. Whether I had myself. I reached into my jacket and pulled out a brown paper bag, damp as if it had once held a broken egg, slipping the Glock inside before tucking it away again. The alley was silent except for the distant hum of the city, indifferent to the violence that had just unfolded. The popcorn seemed finished for the day, no pops.

I knelt down, searching the man's pockets. A crumpled photograph of a young girl, perhaps his daughter, stared back at me. Her eyes were wide with fear, her posture stiff as if she dared not move, like the cameraman was a vicious dog. The image was chilling, the innocence tainted by the terror frozen on her face. I took the photograph, feeling a pang of guilt but knowing it was a necessary evil. The photograph, I left with him, a small piece of his humanity in this desolate place. I picked up the 9mm shell casing and put it in my pocket. I've seen soldiers use them to balance wobbly tables, so it could be useful. As I walked away, I carried a vivid color copy of the girl in my mind. I will carry it forever, a perverse treasure. I lit a cigarette and composed a verse in my mind.

Back in my quarters, I found Ahmad waiting for me. His eyes, always perceptive, took in my worn appearance and the tension in my stance. He didn't ask any questions, just handed me a cup of tea and sat with me in silence.

I hadn't slept in days, my mind racing with thoughts of the explosion, the foot, the little girl. The paranoia and guilt had become constant companions. As I sat in the dimly lit room, staring at the walls, there was a soft knock on the door.

Johny stood there, a stark contrast to the chaos outside. He didn't need to speak; we had shared too many words, too many secrets. He handed me a small bundle of papers. The top sheet had a familiar name: Osiris Mandarin. My alias, my words. Cold sweat beaded on my forehead as I realized the full weight of what I had done.

The papers Johny gave me detailed the Regime's plans, a grim dossier tracing back to the man I'd shot. The one who screamed infidel. He had been more than just a drunk with a knife; he was a hitman for The Regime, sent to silence me and anyone else in his path. The Regime knew about me. They were piecing it together, but they didn't have my name yet. Just the alias. I took the papers, my hands steady but my resolve hardening. I had put us all at risk, but there was no turning back now. The Regime was planning something big. They were looking for me. They wouldn't stop until they found me.

Johny's eyes bore into mine. He didn't need to say more. He was heading back to Texas to lay low. Our paths diverged here, but the mission remained the same. As he turned to leave, he paused at the door, a silent message passing between us. The man I'd killed was part of something larger, and it wasn't over. A man he knew would burn down the whole goddamn world for a little girl. It was a reminder that I wasn't alone in this fight. But it wasn't about hope. It was about finishing what we started.

With Johny gone, I sat back down, the weight of the papers in my hands.

17

THE STING

THE WASP STING marked the end of my husband, for me. It was late afternoon, and Sophie was playing in the garden, her laughter a rare sound in our home's oppressive silence. I sat at the kitchen table, staring at a cold cup of tea, lost in thought. Her cry reached me on a primal, motherly frequency. I would stand between her and anything.

I rushed outside, heart pounding. Sophie was clutching her arm, tears streaming down her face. She pointed shakily at the dying wasp on the ground. Kneeling beside her, my hands trembled as I tried to soothe her and ease her pain.

I gathered her up and carried her inside, her sobs piercing my heart. I called for Jonathan. His study door was slightly ajar, for once. I glanced down the hall and saw him standing there, watching. He had seen it happen. He saw the wasp sting her and heard our daughter cry out in pain. But he remained frozen, as if rooted to the spot.

The wasp sting was a test. It revealed the chasm that had

opened between us. His eyes flickered with something—recognition or perhaps a brief moment of empathy. But then, as quickly as it came, it vanished. He mumbled something about needing to get back to work and retreated into his study, closing the door behind him. The click of the latch was a final, crushing blow.

I sat there, holding Sophie as her sobs quieted to whimpers. The wasp sting, such a small thing, shattered any remaining illusions I had. Jonathan, my husband, was lost to me. He had become a ghost, more comfortable with poetry than with comforting his own daughter.

My husband was like Gregor Samsa, transformed into something unrecognizable, a burden to his family. Once vibrant and engaged, he now seemed as distant and unreachable as Gregor behind his locked door. The tragedy in Kafka's tale was not just in Gregor's transformation, but in his family's inability to see him as he once was.

We were living our own version of Kafka's nightmare. Jonathan's work had become his prison, an impenetrable barrier between him and the world. The man I married, the father of my child, was now a ghost in our home, frozen in place as life continued around him.

The Regime had a way of turning hearts to stone, its whispers filling the air with a quiet dread. Yet, in that cold order, there was a strange comfort. Life under The Regime was predictable, each person a cog in the great machine, their roles clear, the chaos held at bay. Jonathan, in his retreat into the abstract and the poetic, had fled from this order. He found refuge in a realm untouched by The

Regime's reach. But in doing so, he left Sophie and me to face the world alone, unshielded from its harsh realities.

Sophie looked up at me, her eyes wide with confusion and hurt. Where's Daddy? Her voice trembled. I couldn't find the words to explain. How do you tell a child that her father is right there, yet so far gone? How do you explain that he's become a stranger, trapped in a world of his own making?

The wasp sting had laid bare the distance between us. It was a wound that might never heal, a reminder of the man Jonathan once was and the shell he had become. As I held Sophie close, whispering empty reassurances, I felt the weight of our isolation, the silence of 8 Davie Lane pressing in on us.

In the stillness, the idea crept in, unbidden. The Regime's order, its certainty, its clear lines. Jonathan's path seemed more and more like a maze without an exit. The thought of aligning myself with The Regime, of finding some stability, lingered in the back of my mind. It was a quiet betrayal, growing in the dark corners of my heart.

In the end, we were all stung.

18

BERLIN IS A ZIPPER

BERLIN IS DIVIDED like a zipper about to burst, the split between East and West as much ideological as it is physical. The Wall stands as a scar on the collective psyche, a tattooed symbol of the struggle between opposing forces.

I navigate through the shadows of Kreuzberg, the epicenter of dissent. The air is thick with coal smoke and rebellion, leaving everything coated in black. In a dimly lit bar, I gather with comrades, planning our next move against The Regime. We speak in hushed tones, our words heavy with the promise of revolt. Graffiti on cracked walls proclaims our defiance: freedom or death.

One night, as I return to my squat, a crumbling tenement on the verge of collapse, I find an envelope slipped under my door. It's unmarked, except for a single name scrawled in bold, black ink: Osiris Mandarin. Finally. The name is a ghost, a myth among radicals and dreamers. I rip open the envelope, my hands shaking.

The words burrow into my mind, planting seeds of doubt and curiosity. Who am I? What am I fighting for? These questions gnaw at my resolve, shaking the foundations of my beliefs. I pocket the letter and step back into the night, the city a maze of secrets and shadows.

The next evening, I meet my contact on the roof of an abandoned building, its vantage point offering a panoramic view of the Wall. He hands me a dossier filled with coded messages and surveillance photos. As we discuss our plans, a helicopter's searchlight sweeps across the rooftops, forcing us into the shadows.

Beneath Berlin's bustling streets lies a network of tunnels. These dark passages are our sanctuary, a hidden world where plans are made and secrets exchanged. I meet with fellow revolutionaries, their faces obscured in the dim light of flickering lanterns.

Our group's leader, Heinrich Heinz Baumann, is a grizzled veteran of countless battles. His presence is both commanding and unsettling. Heinz is a large, Falstaffian figure with a booming laugh that can fill a room, but his eyes carry the weight of unspeakable horrors.

They broke her. The Regime's police. They took my wife and made her write lies about me. Forced her to pen the words that condemned me.

Heinz reaches into his coat and pulls out a worn piece of paper. He unfolds it carefully, his hands trembling.

I hate her for it. But what choice did she have? They tortured her, broke her spirit. Now she lives, but she is dead to me.

Heinz's voice trembles as he finishes, a tear glistening in

his eye. Before they twisted her words into weapons against us.

He pulls out another piece of paper, this one marked with the harsh, mechanical script of a typewriter. This is what they made her write.

Heinz crumples the paper in his fist, the crackle echoing like someone walking away down a street of broken glass. To see the woman you love reduced to a tool of the enemy? To read her words, knowing they were written under duress, but still feeling the sting of betrayal?

I nod, the gravity of his words sinking in. Heinz is a man forged in the fires of conflict, his soul scarred by loss and betrayal. He is larger than life, yet haunted by the ghosts of his past.

We must be vigilant. The enemy is always watching, always waiting for us to slip. We cannot afford to be careless.

As we disperse into the darkness, I can't shake the feeling that my every move is being scrutinized, every word dissected for hidden meaning. The weight of the letter in my pocket grows heavier, its cryptic message a constant reminder of the fragile line we walk.

In another corner of our underground world, there's Lars, an eccentric poet with a taste for the unusual. He makes chapbooks from soup can labels, writing his poems on the inside and binding them with what he calls Soviet yarn. These labels are remnants of his past, a reminder of his days as a respected professor of literature at the University of Leipzig. The Regime's police had ransacked his apartment, confiscating his books and manuscripts, leaving him with nothing but his wits and an endless supply of soup cans.

Necessity is the mother of invention. They took everything, but they couldn't take my words.

He hands me one of his chapbooks, a small, tattered thing held together by strands of red yarn. The poems inside are wild and unrefined, much like the man himself.

Lars's poems embody resilience, a defiance of the oppressive forces that seek to silence us. He is a poet of the people, his words a weapon in the fight for freedom. His work surfaces at the most opportune moments, passed around like contraband, igniting sparks of hope.

But Lars's past is more tangled than his makeshift books. It's an open secret among our group that he had an affair with Anna before her capture. The knowledge festers, a wound that never quite heals. Heinz and Lars share a space filled with silent contempt and barely concealed rage.

One evening, I found myself between the two men. The tension was palpable, the air heavy with unspoken accusations.

Heinz, you have to let it go. Anna made her own choices.

Heinz's face turned crimson. You dare speak of choices? You seduced her while I fought for our cause. You're a coward and a parasite.

Lars smirked, a bitter edge to his smile. And you think you're a hero? Fighting for a cause that's lost before it began? At least I gave her something to live for, however brief.

Before Heinz could respond, I stepped in, placing a hand on his broad chest. Enough. We have bigger enemies to fight. Save your rage for them.

Heinz glared at Lars one last time before turning away, the conflict unresolved but momentarily defused.

That night, I was supposed to meet Lars to discuss distributing his latest batch of chapbooks. The streets were unusually quiet as I made my way through the narrow alleys of East Berlin. My thoughts were consumed by the bitterness between Heinz and Lars, their animosity a microcosm of our fractured resistance.

As I approached our meeting point, I sensed that I was being followed. I quickened my pace, ducking into a deserted courtyard. From the shadows, a figure emerged, clad in the ominous uniform of The Regime's police.

Osiris Mandarin. We've been expecting you.

I pulled my Makarov from my coat, my heart pounding in my chest. The agent lunged at me, and we grappled in the darkness, our breaths mingling in the cold night air. I pulled the trigger. The agent collapsed, a heap at my feet. I stood over him, my hands shaking, the weight of what I'd done pressing down on me.

I returned to my squat, the envelope and its message pulsing in my pocket. I sat at my makeshift desk, the dim light of a single bulb casting long shadows on the walls. The faces of those I'd lost, those who had fought and died for the cause, haunted me.

In the bar, Dragan sits in a corner, his fingers drumming on the table, a cigarette smoldering between his lips. The smoke curls around him, obscuring his face in a haze of nicotine and shadows. I'd heard of Dragan—brilliant, full of hot air, and always provocative. As I approach, he waves me over with a sly smile.

I slide into the seat opposite him. He leans in, eyes

gleaming with a strange intensity, as if he knows secrets that could unravel the world.

Have you seen The Battle of Algiers? he asks, his voice low and smooth. The moral complexities of resistance, it's all there. Not just the tactics, but the sacrifices, the impossible choices.

He takes a drag from his cigarette, the tip glowing brighter in the dim light. The FLN used brutal tactics—bombings, assassinations. Necessary evils, they would say. But what happens when the line between us and them blurs? When our actions mirror the very oppression we fight against?

His eyes search mine, probing for understanding. He doesn't wait for a response, just keeps talking, weaving a web of thought and smoke.

Think about it, he continues. The Regime shapes our reality, our sense of self. We internalize their control, and in resisting, we risk becoming what we despise. It's like a man looking in a mirror and seeing the monster he's fighting. They manipulate the symbolic order, reshaping our desires and fears, until we don't know where they end and we begin.

He pauses, tapping ash from his cigarette into an over-flowing tray. There was a soldier, he says, killed in the Soviet Union for abandoning his post. They made an example of him. Sacrifices are necessary, but every action has its price.

He leans back, his fingers still drumming. And then there's Osiris Mandarin, he adds, almost as an afterthought. A name that haunts the corridors of resistance, a ghost story we tell ourselves to keep the fear at bay. But who is he, really? A man, a myth, or a collective voice of dissent?

Dragan's fingers drum faster on the table, his eyes flickering with something between excitement and anxiety. Big things are coming, my friend. Morally complex things. We must be prepared to face the consequences, to embrace the chaos that comes with true resistance.

He stands abruptly, placing a hand on my shoulder, his grip firm. Trust your instincts. The mind is the ultimate battlefield.

Berlin is a city split like a zipper ready to burst. Each side thrusts its ideals into the night, and in the midst of this relentless dance, we navigate the shadows, seeking freedom in the cracks of the Wall.

19

BABUSHKA ANYA

THE LANDSCAPE IS a vast expanse of frozen desolation, a white purgatory stretching endlessly under a tarnished silver sky. The air is brittle, piercing each breath, and the wind lashes like an unseen whip. Snow falls incessantly, each flake a silent rebuke to the life struggling beneath it.

A military post stands like a monolith against the elements, but inside its walls, fear holds dominion. Soldiers move with the lethargy of the oppressed, their eyes hollow, their hearts hardened by relentless oppression. The Regime's iron fist is felt in every corner, its presence a suffocating weight on the soul.

Sergei Ivanov mopes among them, a faceless cog in the vast machine. By night, he is not Sergei Ivanov but Osiris Mandarin, a poet whose verses are quiet insurgencies against The Regime's tyranny. In the dim light of his barracks, Sergei carves lines of poetry into the margins of old newspapers. His words fuse despair and defiance, speaking of freedom, unbound dreams, and a world where a man can live and die by his own will. Tucked inside his coat, he carries a precious copy of Gospels in Brief, a gift from his mother when he left for the army. Its presence comforts him, reminding him of gentler times and unwavering faith.

Paris smolders with unrest and opportunity, but that's another tale. Here, in this frozen wasteland, Sergei feels the cold embrace tightening around his soul. Every breath is a battle, every day a skirmish against creeping numbness that threatens to claim him.

One moonless night, driven by a yearning for freedom stronger than fear of death, Sergei makes his escape. He slips past the guards, his heart pounding with the rhythm of his own daring. The frozen wilderness welcomes him with icy arms, and he stumbles through the snow, each step marking his defiance.

Days pass in a blur of cold and hunger. The wilderness is merciless, and Sergei's strength wanes. But fate, capricious and cruel, guides him to a small, isolated cabin, a lone glimmer amidst the vast expanse, inhabited by an old woman named Babushka Anya, whose face is a map of wrinkles and whose eyes harbor a silent promise of treachery.

Babushka Anya takes him in, offering warmth and a simple meal of cabbage soup. Sergei shares his poetry, and she listens with a smile that never reaches her eyes. She is nurturing, yet her gaze holds untold secrets. She feeds him, her hands steady, her voice a soft murmur of old folk tales blending with Sergei's dreams.

In the dim light of a single candle, Sergei writes. His poetry flows from his pen like blood from a wound, dark and introspective, reflecting the bleakness of his situation. Yet there is a spark of hope, revealing his unyielding spirit. He writes of the cold, the silence, the unforgiving land that mirrors the desolation within his heart.

The bond between Sergei and Babushka Anya grows. She is a silent witness to his torment, a vessel for his words. Her cabin becomes a place his soul can breathe, a retreat where his verses can come to life. He often reads from Gospels in Brief, drawing strength from its passages.

But shadows of duplicity are ever-present. One frigid morning, Sergei awakens to the sound of heavy boots outside the cabin. Babushka Anya stands at the door with Regime soldiers. Her smile is gone, her eyes cold and distant as they push past her into the cabin.

Colonel Viktor Orlov steps forward. His thick, dark mustache frames a mouth set in a perpetual scowl, bushy eyebrows shadow his piercing eyes, and his stern face is marked by the hard lines of power. He exudes an air of authority that brooks no dissent.

Comrade Ivanov, he begins, his voice a study in practiced conviction, you have betrayed The Regime by fleeing your post. But do not fear, for even in your defection, the Party remains just and merciful. We shall bring you back into the fold, and you will learn the error of your ways.

The soldiers seize him, ignoring his protests, his verses swallowed by the icy silence. They drag him away, the snow muffling his cries. As they lead him, Sergei clutches his coat, feeling the worn cover of the small book hidden inside.

Sergei is led to a stone wall, the cold biting through his resolve. The men around him are unyielding, their eyes as cold as the wind. He stands before the wall, a solitary figure against the white expanse.

Colonel Orlov steps up to Sergei, continuing his monologue. Understand, Comrade Ivanov, The Regime is the guiding light of hope and equality for all mankind. Your individualistic pursuits, your poetry, are distractions from the collective good. The strength of The Regime lies in our unity, our common purpose.

He pauses, then adds with a smirk, you should be proud, even in this moment, to contribute to the greater good, to the strength of our Motherland.

As they prepare him for execution, Sergei mutters lines of poetry, clinging to his identity as Osiris Mandarin until the very end. His verses are his shield, his final act of defiance against the world that seeks to silence him.

Colonel Orlov gives the order, and the shots ring out. Sergei's final words are lost to the wind, his body collapsing into the snow. The cold claims him, his life extinguished, but his spirit remains unbroken. The small book falls from his coat, its pages fluttering in the frigid air.

After the execution, Babushka Anya approaches Colonel Orlov, offering him a bowl of cabbage soup. Her eyes are downcast, her hands trembling as she holds out the bowl. The officer accepts the soup, the warmth a stark contrast to the coldness of their actions.

Babushka Anya returns to her cabin, her expression an enigma, her motives a mystery. She sits by the fire, the flickering flames casting shadows on the walls. In her hands, she holds a piece of paper, Sergei's final poem. She reads it silently, her eyes filling with unshed tears.

The wind howls outside, a mournful dirge for the lost and the forgotten. The cabin stands alone, a solitary witness to fleeting moments of defiance and despair. Babushka Anya remains, a guardian of secrets, a keeper of stories. The flames flicker, the shadows dance, and the cabin stands, a silent witness to the tale of Osiris Mandarin, the poet whose words were swallowed by the cold, whose spirit struggled against the icy desolation, a faint light in a land of endless night.

She writes a message inside the front cover of Gospels in Brief. It is a simple note: Osiris Mandarin is dead. Now she must get the book to Prague.

20

PRAGUE BOOKSELLER

THE BOOKSTORE on a quiet street in Prague was a refuge for the soul, hidden within the folds of history. Shadows whispered secrets, and the scent of old paper clung to the air like a ghost. To a casual observer, it was merely a repository of forgotten knowledge. But to the resistance, it was a crucial link, a hidden artery pumping the blood of rebellion through a city strangled by The Regime.

I was its keeper, a night watchman of words and whispers, a guardian of forbidden knowledge. Once, I had been a professor, teaching literature at Charles University. Kafka and Kundera were my realm, exploring human absurdity and existential despair was my calling. However, The Regime had no tolerance for probing such dark corners of the human psyche. My lectures on the absurdity of life, the futility of resistance, and society's inevitable decay were deemed subversive. The irony was not lost on me.

By day, I moved among the aisles of my shop with the

ease of a man at peace with his solitary existence. By night, the place transformed. Shadows grew deeper, and the air thickened with the scent of despair and defiance. The bookstore was my cave, and I was its solitary guardian, watching over a hidden flame that flickered despite The Regime's attempts to snuff it out.

The bell above the door chimed softly, a reminder that even in the darkest of times, life goes on. A familiar face appeared—Marek, the resistance courier, stepped into the dim light of the shop. His presence was a cold gust of reality, stark against the warmth of old books and whispered secrets.

Marek moved with precision, his eyes sharp, his face a mask of stone. He approached the counter, his footsteps silent on the worn wooden floor. In his hands, he carried a plain brown paper bag.

He placed the bag on the counter with a deliberate motion, his eyes meeting mine briefly. There was no need for words. Marek's silence filled the space between us. Without a sound, he slid the brown paper package toward me.

I took it, feeling the weight of its contents. Inside, I knew, was something important—something that needed to be kept safe. I opened the package and pulled out a book— Gospels in Brief. The familiar cover brought a sense of nostalgia and unease. Marek's impassive gaze lingered on me as I opened the book.

Inside the front cover, written in neat handwriting, was the message: Osiris Mandarin is dead. The message was in Babushka Anya's hand.

I looked up at Marek, searching for any sign of emotion, but his face remained impassive. He had delivered the news with the same detachment as he had the package. There was no reaction, no flicker of feeling. He was a stone-cold courier, a man who had seen too much and learned to show nothing.

Marek gave a brief nod, acknowledging the receipt of the message, then turned to leave. His work here was done. He moved toward the door with the same silent efficiency, a ghost slipping back into the shadows.

As the door closed behind him, the bell chimed softly again, a reminder of the relentless passage of time. I stood there, holding the book, the weight of the news settling over me. The death of Sergei, the man behind Osiris Mandarin, was a crushing blow to the resistance, a reminder of the constant danger we faced.

But the book in my hands was also a symbol of hope. Sergei's words would live on, inspiring others to continue the fight.

The bell above the door chimed softly, and I looked up to see another customer. Another day in the life of a bookseller. But beneath the surface, a revolution was brewing, one that would not be silenced. I took a final drag from my cigarette and stepped forward, ready to face whatever came next. Now I had to get the book to Berlin.

21

___

RED DRAGON CAFÉ

THE RED DRAGON CAFÉ was a haven of shadows and silence. The air was thick with the scent of soy and garlic. I pushed through the door and made my way inside, passing Andrei at a corner table. His voice was a low murmur under the dim glow of lanterns. Lacan speaks of the real, the symbolic, the imaginary, he droned. The crowd was captivated, faces illuminated by flickering candlelight. I watched, a silent observer, my skepticism sharpening.

I found a seat at the bar, ordered a glass of the house red, and grimaced as the liquid hit my tongue. It was an insult to wine, barely drinkable. I turned to Raymond Carver, who sat beside me nursing his own drink, eyes bloodshot and distant.

Ray, how do you stomach this swill

Carver barely acknowledged me, lost in his own world. Iowa Writers' Workshop, he mumbled. Found the file at Iowa. Gardner, the same guy who wrote Grendel? Yeah, always talking about the ethics of fiction, but it was all about control. A way to shape the narrative.

I nodded more out of habit than agreement. Carver's ramblings were a familiar refrain, a background hum to the night's oppressive ambiance. My focus shifted back to Andrei, whose grandiose proclamations continued unabated.

The door swung open, and in walked a man with a wild beard and eyes that burned with intensity. Dragan exuded manic energy. He was a tormented poet, a modern-day prophet amidst the din of the café. Women turned to look, more interested in his fervor than any physical appeal. Even Andrei's spotlight dimmed in his presence.

I watched as Dragan made his way to Andrei's table. The two exchanged words, their conversation a blend of conspiracy and ideology. Andrei gestured for me to join them, a flicker of excitement in his eyes.

I took my glass and moved to their table, settling into the seat next to Andrei. Dragan gave me a curt nod, his eyes scanning me with a mixture of curiosity and calculation.

Amnon Mint, Andrei introduced me with a flourish. The novelist himself.

I inclined my head, acknowledging the introduction with a hint of amusement. Dragan's presence intrigued me, but my skepticism remained.

So, Amnon, Dragan said, your book on the Paris jazz scene. Interesting read.

Interesting? I arched an eyebrow. Not exactly a glowing endorsement.

Dragan shrugged, a ghost of a smile playing on his lips.

Dubois, the jazz musician you wrote about. Did you know he was killed by The Regime?

I stared at him, my mind racing. Dubois's death had always been shrouded in mystery, but I had never considered such a sinister end. Dragan's assertion added a new layer to the story, transforming Dubois from a tragic figure into a martyr.

You're saying The Regime had him killed? I couldn't keep the incredulity from my voice.

Dragan nodded, eyes alight with conviction. His music was subversive. It spoke to the people, ignited a fire The Regime couldn't control. They silenced him to prevent that fire from spreading.

As he spoke, I saw him and Andrei as modern-day zealots, their fervor rivaling early Christian evangelists. These men were apostles of resistance, preaching their doctrine with religious intensity.

Their zeal drove them forward but also blinded them to more nuanced truths. They were so caught up in their crusade that they failed to see the broader picture, the intricate web of causes and effects shaping our world.

Were they truly fighting for freedom, or simply enamored with their own sense of importance? Like early evangelists, they were driven by belief and a desire for validation. It was a stark reminder of the lengths true believers would go to suppress dissent, to silence any voice that dared challenge their doctrine.

As Dragan continued to speak, I saw them for what they were: modern-day apostles of a nascent religion, their gospel one of resistance and revolution. They were as much a product of their times as the early Christians, caught in a struggle about identity and purpose as much as politics. Their passion was undeniable, but so too was their fanaticism, and it made me wary.

Their stories would make for compelling material, but I would have to tread carefully, separating truth from fervent embellishments. The novel I envisioned would capture their narrative and their zealotry, the line between conviction and fanaticism that defined their lives. It was a story that needed to be told, but it would be my story, shaped by my judgment.

As Dragan's voice droned on about resistance and revolution, my mind wandered. The air in the Red Dragon Café felt thicker, weighed down by their convictions. I needed to clear my head, to step away from the oppressive atmosphere.

I glanced at my watch. Midnight was approaching. Andrei caught my eye and gave a barely perceptible nod, signaling our meeting was drawing to a close. I stood up, pushing my chair back slowly, my thoughts shifting to the night ahead.

Stepping outside, the cool air washed over me, a stark contrast to the heat inside. The streets were quiet, the city holding its breath. I walked aimlessly, replaying the fervent words exchanged in the café. The sense of unease lingered, a premonition of something yet to come.

In the distance, a clock chimed, its sound reverberating through the empty streets. Midnight. Somewhere in the city, a decision was being made, a plan set into motion.

22

NAMELESS ROOF

THE AIR IS cold and clear atop this nameless roof. I settle into the city's low hum, laying prone behind my Dragunov sniper rifle. A Makarov pistol sits in a paper bag beside me, along with a piece of cheese and a bottle of milk. The simplicity of my sustenance contrasts with the precision of my task.

Through the scope, I stare into the darkness of an apartment. The lights are out, with only a sporadic flash of a cigarette ember breaking the void. Each ember flickers and fades. Occasionally, a match flares, its sudden brightness disturbing my night vision.

The ember takes me back to nights hunting with my father. The air thick with humidity and fireflies, memories now tainted by inevitability. He taught me patience, silence, the certainty of death. Life is a series of endings, each a prelude to the next. Schopenhauer's philosophy became my creed—life is a constant process of dying.

A gust of wind pulls me back. The city below holds its

breath, waiting. Hours to go before dawn. I take a bite of cheese, the taste bland but necessary. My scope remains fixed on the dark window, the solitary ember my only companion.

I pull out a cigarette and light it under a small tarp, hiding the glow inside a beer can as I smoke. Each inhale is a momentary respite from the anticipation. The ember at the end of my cigarette mirrors the one in the apartment, a solitary point of light in the darkness. The smoke curls around me, mingling with the city's unseen breath.

Time stretches thin. I must be gone before dawn. My target, Viktor, who once ran The Kraken tattoo studio, now hides in that apartment. He used to have a beard like Vladimir Solov'ev, but he's changed his appearance. Intelligence suggests he's hiding from The Regime. My mind estimates an 85 percent chance that the ember is my quarry.

The Kraken was more than a tattoo parlor; it was a haven for those who wore their defiance on their skin. It was where I got my own tattoo, a small insignia marking me as one of the initiated.

I remember the first time I walked into The Kraken. The scent of ink and disinfectant mixed with heavy smoke, the sound of the tattoo needle constant. Viktor had a quiet intensity. While he inked my skin, he spoke of Osiris Mandarin with reverence. Osiris is not just a man, he said. He is a symbol, a guiding star for those who seek truth and freedom. His poetry can shake any regime.

Tell me more about him. Who is he really?

Osiris Mandarin is a pseudonym, a mask worn by many. In Paris, he was Jean-Luc, a cigarette-smoking neurotic revolutionary. In Moscow, he was Sergei, a disillusioned poet. Each incarnation carries the same spirit, the same defiance.

A distant siren wails, pulling me back. The wind blows west. I adjust my scope, calculating the variables. No room for dilemmas, only success. I light another cigarette, hiding the glow inside the beer can. Each drag reminds me of the stakes, a calm before the storm. Schopenhauer often said, The world is my representation. Here, my world is reduced to this single frame, a window into a man's ritual. I consider the probabilities, the rhythms of the puffs. The silhouette moves, shifting and melding into the shadows. Chance dances on the precipice of my aim.

Another memory, a basement in Prague. 1968, the air thick with revolution. Pavel, an underground publisher, showed me a leaflet, a poem by Osiris Mandarin. The authorities fear him, Pavel said. His words are more dangerous than any weapon. They can't control his ideas.

I read the poem, each line striking at oppression's heart. It was clear why The Regime wanted him silenced. Osiris Mandarin was a threat to their existence.

The cigarette ember glows again. Hours have passed, yet I am no closer to seeing his face. The anticipation gnaws at me. If I fail, I won't get another chance. The city will awaken soon, and with it, the eyes of The Regime.

Dawn creeps closer. A conversation in a cramped apartment in Moscow comes to mind. Sergei spoke of art's power to resist. Art is the last refuge of the free, he said. When everything else is taken, art remains. It is the soul's defiance.

Viktor gave me a tattoo of a raven inside a labyrinth. A symbol of freedom within constraints. I often wonder if my work, my cold precision, is a form of art. Each mission a brushstroke, each target a canvas. Tonight, as I watch the ember flicker and fade, I question the morality of my art.

The wind howls. I squeeze the trigger. The silence shatters. The apartment window breaks apart in a spray of glass and screams. Below, a man yells about lightning.

I remain still, the weight of inevitability settling over me. The ember is extinguished. Darkness is absolute once more. I pack my Dragunov and slip the Makarov into my coat. The cheese, with one bite taken, and the milk, untouched, serve as reminders of the night's focus.

As I descend the building, Schopenhauer's words haunt me: Life is a constant process of dying. In this city, I am but a shadow, an instrument of The Regime. The poet Osiris Mandarin's voice is silenced, and with it, a piece of resistance and beauty is lost forever.

My footsteps whisper against the concrete, a calculated retreat. The city sprawls beneath me, a desolate smear of lights and shadows. It breathes with the rhythm of hidden lives, each one a potential story, a potential target.

As I move through the streets, my senses are attuned to every sound, every flicker of movement. The city's pulse is my own, a silent symphony of survival. I pass a street vendor setting up for the morning rush, the smell of fresh bread mingling with the air. A Lenin statue looms over the square, a reminder of The Regime's watchful eye. It reminds me of simpler times, a life abandoned for this path of shadows and silence.

I light another cigarette, inhaling deeply. The smoke mingles with the morning air, a transient veil briefly obscuring harsh reality. Memories come unbidden, fragments of a life in the dark. Each mission, each target, a brushstroke on my existence. I think of Berlin, Viktor, and his tattoos of resistance. I think of Pavel in Prague, distributing Osiris Mandarin's forbidden words. Each one a part of a larger picture, a web spanning continents and ideologies.

I reach my temporary safe house, a small room above a butcher's shop. The scent of raw meat is overpowering, but it's a small price for anonymity. I clean my Dragunov meticulously, each motion a ritual of precision. The Makarov, still in its paper bag, is a silent companion, a reminder of life's fragility and death's certainty. The cheese, with one bite taken, and the milk, untouched, are reminders of the night's grim fulfillment.

I lie on the cot, exhaustion seeping into my bones. Sleep comes slowly, haunted by past ghosts and the future's inevitability. In this city, I am but a shadow, an instrument of The Regime. The poet's words may be silenced, but their impact will remain in the shadows, a reminder of existence's fleeting nature.

I awaken with a start. The room is dark, save for the faint glow of the streetlight. The quiet is oppressive, a stark contrast to last night's commotion. The mission's completion is both a relief and a burden. The weight lingers, a heavy blanket over my soul.

I walk to the window, looking out. The city is a place where beauty and brutality coexist. I watch the first light of dawn break, casting long shadows. A new day, but for me, just another step in the process of dying.

I gather my things. The rifle is carefully disassembled

and packed. The Makarov returns to my coat. The cheese and milk, untouched except for one bite, are left on the table as a silent reminder. I take one last look around, ensuring no trace remains.

Stepping into the cool morning air, I feel detached. The city wakes up, unaware of the darkness it harbors. I am a ghost, a phantom moving unseen through the world. It's a lonely existence, one I have chosen, aligning with my philosophy and purpose.

I light another cigarette. Memories come unbidden. Each mission, each target, reminds me of my path. The faces of those I have silenced haunt me.

Osiris Mandarin's poetry is now just a memory. His words, though silenced, will continue to inspire and incite. His legacy, carried by those who knew him, will endure. My actions, while necessary, are a small part of a larger struggle. The resistance will continue, the fight for freedom and truth unending.

In this city, I am but a shadow, an instrument of The Regime. The poet's words may be silenced, but their impact endures, a testament to the human spirit.

I finish my cigarette, extinguishing the ember under my boot. I am a ghost, a phantom. A lonely existence, one I have chosen. My work is far from over. The shadows still have many stories to tell. And I will be there, a silent witness, a calculating instrument in the hands of fate.

23

NEW YORK LIBRARY

THE LIBRARY AT NIGHT BREATHES, silence broken by the creak of old wooden shelves and the rustle of forgotten knowledge. Dust motes drift in flickering candlelight, casting twisting shadows. This place, both refuge and prison, is my sanctuary. I wander the dim aisles, insomnia pressing down like a curse. My calloused hands glide over the spines of rare, out-of-print books on philosophy and music theory. These volumes offer truths without judgment, unlike the deceitful people outside. In the stillness of the stacks, ghosts whisper, forgotten dreams linger in the scent of aged pages, mocking my existence.

Detroit feels like another life, a distant memory of Motown, my father's labor at the auto plant, my mother's hymns, the nights at the piano, fingers dancing over worn keys. I was young, dreaming of New York City, the Blue Note, the applause. The spiral into addiction was quick and merciless. Jazz took me high, then dropped me low. But Paris was supposed to be my redemption.

I found myself in the smoky haze of Parisian jazz clubs like Le Caveau de la Huchette and Le Duc des Lombards. My trumpet sang songs of pain and joy, and the people listened. I played alongside names like Bud Powell, Lucky Thompson, and Kenny Clarke. For a while, it was enough. But the world was on fire. Regimes rising, freedoms falling. My music became a quiet rebellion, a whisper of resistance. I played with words and notes, collaborated with poets and activists. Osiris Mandarin, they called me. It felt powerful, like I could change something.

Then, they came for me. I knew they would. The Regime doesn't tolerate dissent, not even in jazz. I disappeared that night, the city holding its breath, thinking I was dead. It was easier that way. But dead men can't play, can't fight, can't feel.

Now, I am a ghost in this library, far from the lights of Paris. I guard these books, these fragile vessels of knowledge and history. Each one a piece of a world that was, and maybe, a world that could be again. The flask of bourbon in my locker offers small comfort. Books are my solace; people lie and judge, but books are honest. My poetry, written in the margins, imagines readers discovering my words long after I'm gone, craving connection but only from a distance.

Margaret, the library's supervisor, brings me cookies, her gaze lingering too long, her smile too warm. I nod and thank her, but the cookies end up behind the library where the stray cats gather. I read my poetry aloud to the cats, indifferent and accepting. Lately, the feeling of being watched grows, shadows shift, eyes follow. Notes appear in the margins of the books where I write my poetry, responding to my words, calling me Osiris Mandarin. Paranoia becomes a constant hum.

Dragan sent a note through a resistance courier, Marek. Amnon Mint, the author who declared me dead in his book, was now considering writing about Osiris Mandarin. Dragan's note suggested Mint might be looking to uncover more about the myths surrounding me. It was time to act.

I decided to reach out to Mint. He needed to know the truth, to understand what really happened. Writing the letter was an act of defiance, every word a strike against the silence that has suffocated me for so long. I told him to meet me at The Kraken, an old haunt, a place where the past and present could intersect. I chose a date two weeks from now, giving him enough time to make arrangements, but not enough to overthink or alert unwanted attention.

As I sealed the letter, my hands were steady with purpose. Walking to the mailbox felt like crossing a threshold, leaving behind the shadows and stepping into the light. This letter is my first act of rebellion in years, a signal to The Regime that I am still here, still fighting.

24

TUCSON

THE TUCSON HEAT simmered with the burden I carried. My office, a mess of analytic philosophy and half-finished poetry, reflected my inner confusion. The scent of weed and old paper lingered, symbolizing my rebellion against traditional academia. Rolling a joint with a page from Kant's Critique captured my disdain for dogma and myself. In those hazy, pre-lecture moments, I found a brief escape, while my students, amused by my quirks, remained unaware of the emptiness I felt.

One night, seeking relief from the relentless heat, I wandered into The Blue Moon bar. The dim lights cast long shadows, blending with the smoke that lazily curled toward the ceiling. Bill Evans played softly, each note a fragment of forgotten dreams I never had.

As I sipped my beer, I noticed Red O'Connor at the bar. A songwriter waiting around to die, he now crackled with unusual energy, talking to the bartender with urgency. I moved closer, pretending to be engrossed in my beer's label.

Red handed the bartender a brown paper bag, which was accepted without question. Once the bartender moved on, I approached Red. He said the bag contained writings by Osiris Mandarin, a mysterious underground poet and philosopher. Red believed these writings held hidden messages that could expose The Regime.

Red got awkward for a second, telling me not to think he was weird. I played it off, saying I didn't think he was too weird, acting like I was joking.

Hearing the name Osiris Mandarin took me back to grad school. I wrote about Shadows of Existence one semester in a metaphysics seminar, not from genuine philosophical interest but because the only girl in the class carried the book around. High and eager to impress her, I wrote a paper titled The Ontological Status of Osiris Mandarin. I argued that Mandarin's work transcended literature, entering the realm of metaphysical inquiry, suggesting his writings actively shaped reality. It was an absurdly grandiose idea, more a product of weed than wisdom.

The professor said it was interesting, though I didn't take it seriously. It earned me a reputation for pushing boundaries, yet left me puzzled why anyone would see Mandarin as more than a curiosity. I moved on, dismissing it as youthful folly.

Red's passionate account now stirred a mix of nostalgia and skepticism. He mentioned Amnon Mint, who was working on a book to decode messages within Shadows of

Existence. Mint believed these writings could reveal hidden truths and expose The Regime. Mint was heading to Berlin, following the resistance.

Despite my skepticism, a strange pull toward the mystery lingered. If these writings could uncover something significant, it was worth investigating. The Regime's shadow loomed even here, in Tucson's smoky corners.

The next morning, I felt a renewed sense of purpose mixed with doubt. The heat pressed down like a weight I couldn't shake. Townes Van Zandt said he'd join me. We packed our bags, the promise of revolution heavy in the air. Berlin awaited, a city draped in shadows and secrets. We were ready to uncover them, whatever the cost.

Returning to The Blue Moon for a final drink before leaving, I noticed an older man at the bar. His posture was rigid, eyes scanning the room with practiced wariness. He approached the bartender, who handed him a brown paper bag. Their conversation was inaudible over the jazz and murmured conversations, but their body language was telling. The man's presence was commanding, his movements precise and calculated.

A waitress drifted by, and I ordered a drink, shifting slightly in my seat to better observe. The older man's presence was unsettling. Each word I caught—operation, compromised—was a shard, piecing together a picture of hidden machinations and looming threats.

Their conversation ended abruptly. The older man stood, leaving a few bills on the bar. Instead of heading straight for the door, he turned and walked toward me. My heart rate quickened, and I hoped my interest hadn't been too obvious.

He slid into the seat across from me, his presence immediately filling the small booth. He introduced himself as Roger Huxley, his voice smooth but edged, suggesting he was not one to be trifled with. His reputation, whispered in circles of those involved in covert operations and hidden truths, was as dark and tangled as the smoke that filled the room.

Huxley mentioned monitoring activities in Tucson and keeping an eye on Red. He noted my position at the university, philosophy professor—a fitting role given our discussion. No small talk, no pleasantries. His words were measured, each one a calculated step in our interaction.

Huxley's presence was a stark contrast to the bar's usual patrons. His air of authority and the way he commanded attention were unsettling. He finished his drink and stood, leaving me to mull over his words. Our paths, he hinted, would cross again.

As he walked away, the bar seemed to thaw, the tension melting like ice in water. But the encounter replayed in my mind, each detail etched in sharp relief. The world outside felt different, charged with the knowledge that beneath the surface, currents were shifting, pulling us all toward an uncertain future.

I watched him leave, the door closing softly behind him. The bar returned to its usual murmur of conversations and jazz, but a shadow lingered. Whatever business Huxley had in Tucson, it would ripple through my life, pulling me deeper into a web of hidden truths and dangerous secrets.

The desert winds whispered their secrets, the night offered no solace, only more questions. I walked the quiet streets, each step heavy with the weight of what I had witnessed. The heat pressed down, as if trying to squeeze the truth out of me. I didn't know what Red and Huxley were involved in, but I knew it was only a matter of time before it touched my life. The shadows of the past were long, and in Tucson, they seemed to stretch forever.

25

OREGON

THE WIND outside the cabin never stops, carrying the scent of pine and the whispers of the forest. Shadows play in the candlelight, casting twisted shapes on the rough wooden walls. This place is both my refuge and my torment.

I sit at my desk, unfinished poems scattered around, each one a fragment of a truth I'm too afraid to fully unveil. The lies I tell in my poetry are easier. The audience demands deception, and I deliver, hating myself with every word.

My mother's voice cuts through the wind's howl, slurred by gin. Stupid boy, she mutters, the alcohol thick on her breath. I answer with silence, politeness masking my contempt. Her father beat her, I remind myself, trying to justify her cruelty.

In the glovebox of my truck, a brown paper bag conceals a Glock 19. It's a relic from my past, a necessary evil in this world of shadows. The forest around the cabin is dense and unforgiving. I wander its paths, the rustling leaves and the wind in the trees my only companions. Paranoia follows me, a constant shadow.

One night, as darkness fell and the forest seemed to close in, I sensed them—masked men moving silently through the trees. Fear gripped me, cold and familiar. I stumbled to the truck, retrieving the Glock with trembling hands. The first shot was a warning, the sound shattering the stillness. The men halted, uncertainty rippling through their ranks. I fired again, closer this time. They retreated, shadows dissolving into the darkness. Relief washed over me, mingling with lingering fear.

Back in the cabin, the candles flickered, their flames a soothing balm to my frayed nerves. I sat at the desk, the blank page before me a challenge and a curse. The need to write, to create, battled with the fear of truth. I picked up my pen, the weight of lies heavy in my hand.

What did they want? The question gnawed at me, an unwelcome intruder in my thoughts. Burglars, perhaps, searching for hidden valuables in a place that held none. Or maybe something more sinister, seeking the man who once uncovered secrets others wanted buried. The paranoia, always lurking, whispered darker possibilities. Were they hired to silence me, to erase the remnants of my once-promising career?

In the small towns of the Pacific Northwest, bookstores smell of must and forgotten dreams. I used to sit in the corner, lighting cigarettes, thumbing through old philosophy texts. Sartre's Nausea spoke to my existential dread, each line resonating with my disillusionment. I remember one passage vividly, where Roquentin describes the feeling of the world's absurdity pressing down on him. I was just thinking that here we are eating and drinking to preserve our precious existence, and that there's nothing, nothing, absolutely no reason for existing.

That line struck me, a bitter truth I've tried to escape. Once, after a night of drinking, I found myself stumbling through the forest, the wind whispering secrets I was too drunk to comprehend. I tripped over a log, falling hard, my lip splitting open against a rock. Needing stitches, I rummaged through my bag and found a needle and thread I had taken from a Holiday Inn in California, remnants of a past trip. Under the dim light of a single candle, I stitched my own lip. Roquentin was right.

Years ago, I wandered through Germany, tracing the steps of Goethe. I felt a kinship with Faust, the man who sold his soul and got nothing in return. My poetry, my supposed genius, all seemed like empty promises. I traded my truth for acceptance, only to find that acceptance was a hollow prize. It was like Robert Johnson at the crossroads, trading his soul for the blues. Only, instead of soulful melodies, I was left with hollow words. I played my part, a poet in disguise, but the cost was my very essence.

I am Osiris Mandarin. The name carved into the stone in that quiet German town where secrets hide in plain sight. They followed me from there, those masked men, shadows from a past I cannot escape. The Regime, perhaps, or something darker, more insidious. Their intentions obscure, but their presence undeniable. Love is a fiction, I reminded myself. The world is a cold place, each person alone in their illusions. I opened my eyes, the pen moving across the page, each word a step closer to the truth I feared. The wind and the flames, constant companions in my solitude, whispered their approval.

One afternoon, in a small bookstore in town, I found myself drawn to the section on revolutionary literature. The scent of old paper and ink filled the air, a comforting reminder of countless hours spent lost in the stacks. As I picked up a hardback about the statistical physics of revolutionary movements, I noticed a familiar figure a few feet away, leafing through a similar volume. It was Ray Carver, the writer whose short stories had once filled me with a mixture of admiration and envy.

Ray swayed slightly as he moved closer, his eyes bloodshot and unfocused. He clutched a book on the Spanish Civil War, his fingers gripping the edges as if it were his only anchor. I watched him from the corner of my eye, my own book suddenly feeling lighter, less substantial.

He stumbled, knocking a pile of books to the floor. The thud broke the silence, drawing the attention of the few patrons scattered among the aisles. I moved to help him, but he waved me off, his gaze locking onto mine for a brief moment. In his eyes, I saw my own desperation, a silent plea for understanding.

Ray managed to gather the scattered volumes, his movements clumsy but determined. He placed the last one back on the shelf, then turned and staggered toward the exit, his presence like a ghost fading into the daylight.

Back in the cabin, the encounter with Ray haunted me. I sat at my desk, the book on revolutionary movements open before me, but my thoughts were elsewhere. The image of

Ray, his bloodshot eyes and trembling hands, lingered in my memory. I picked up my pen, determined to capture the essence of our meeting, to understand the deeper meaning behind it. As I wrote, the lines blurred between my reality and his, our lives intertwined in a dance of desperation and hope.

I recall my first encounter with Sartre's Nausea, the way Roquentin's nausea felt just like my own existential dread. I am. I exist, I think, therefore I am, I muttered to myself, feeling the weight of the world's absurdity pressing down on me. I turned to Camus, seeking solace in his exploration of the human condition. Each line I read deepened my understanding of the futility and beauty of life's struggle.

The cabin sits on the edge of a dense forest, its rough wooden walls a stark contrast to the smooth trunks of the ancient trees. Each creak of the floorboards underfoot breaks the silence, emphasizing the solitude that envelops this place. The fire in the hearth crackles softly, casting flickering shadows that dance across the walls. Outside, the wind rustles through the leaves, a constant, whispering companion.

Memories of my mother's voice, sharp and filled with contempt, intrude on my thoughts. Stupid boy, she would say, the stench of gin heavy in the air. I recall the nights I would hide in my room, listening to her rage against a world that had beaten her down. Her father's fists had left invisible scars, shaping her into the bitter woman she became. The cycle of cruelty continued, leaving me haunted by the remnants of her words.

The masked men are a constant presence in my mind, their silent movements through the trees a reminder
of the threats that lurk in the shadows. Each night, as darkness falls,
my senses heighten. The snap of a
twig, the rustle of leaves, every
sound becomes a potential danger.
My hand trembles as I reach for the
Glock, its cold weight a small
comfort in this world of uncertainty. The first shot echoes in the
stillness, a warning to those who
would dare approach. The shadows
retreat, but the fear remains,
coiling tightly around my thoughts.

As I finished the last lines of my poem, I felt a sense of completion, as if I had captured a fragment of truth. The wind outside continued to howl, the shadows continued to dance, and the candles continued to flicker. The world remained a cold, harsh place, but in the silence of the wind and the glow of the candles, I found a semblance of peace. My words, my lies, my truths—all part of the same fragile existence.

26

IOWA

BEFORE, when I was myself, I taught poetry at the Iowa Writers' Workshop. Though it seemed prestigious, it hid a dark truth. Shadowy powers with ties to The Regime controlled it, aiming to create propaganda and develop mind control techniques. We were mere tools, crafting words that twisted and manipulated thoughts.

Then, the scandal broke. Harsh accusations claimed I had submitted others' work as my own. The poems were similar to those in a book I had found in an East German bookstore, Shadows of Existence. The copy was in German, and I thought no one in America would recognize it. I published them because they felt like my words.

I found solace in a dimly lit bar on South Clinton Street, where the air was thick with smoke and muted conversations. This place became my refuge. I sat at a corner table, scribbling on napkins and scraps of paper, fueled by cheap whiskey and a relentless drive to capture the essence of iden-

tity. Yet, even now, I'm unsure whether the words were truly
my own.

My office at the Workshop, in a Quonset hut, buzzed with
a frequency designed to read and influence thoughts. Overhead lights hummed at exactly 11,249 Hz. These lights,
combined with electromagnetic oscillators and quantum
resonance amplifiers, created a field that interacted with the
brain's synaptic pathways. They turned our minds into open
books for those who knew how to read them. The device
rewired my hippocampus. I could no longer read iambic
pentameter; Shakespeare's words became a cataracted smear,
a swirling vortex of disjointed hieroglyphs and dark
shadows.

Roger Huxley, a colleague, was more than just a poet.
During World War II, he served as an officer in the OSS, the
precursor to the CIA. He had a limp or pretended to. Huxley
was an enigma wrapped in shadows, always lighting cigarettes but never taking a drag. His presence was like a storm
cloud, dark and unpredictable, ready to strike at any
moment.

One night, Raymond Carver, drunker than a poet ought
to be, stumbled into my office. His breath reeked of bourbon,
and his eyes were glassy with regret. He collapsed into a
chair, his words slurred but urgent. Charles, you ever wonder
why the Workshop's so special? he muttered, leaning in
close. It's not just the talent. It's the backing. The money. The
power.

I offered him another drink, and he continued, each word
a revelation. Carver confessed he was working for The
Regime, part of their covert operation to influence American

literature and culture. His stories, seemingly mundane and filled with the minutiae of everyday life, were laced with subtle propaganda, designed to mold minds and manipulate emotions. We're all part of it, he said, his voice steadying. They got us all spinning their webs, telling their stories. It's all a lie.

We took his motorcycle, a rickety beast that groaned under the weight of its secrets. He drove, drunk and reckless, through the empty fields outside town. The wind howled in our ears, a pack of warnings and regrets. We reached a dirt road, barely a path, leading to a solitary cherry tree standing like a sentinel against the darkening sky.

Carver dismounted and stumbled to the base of the tree. He dug into the earth with his bare hands, cursing under his breath. After a few minutes, he uncovered the old ammo can, the paint chipped and rusting. Inside were his poems, his true work, hidden from prying eyes. But it wasn't just poems. Inside the ammo can were notes, maps, letters, each piece more incriminating than the last. They told a story of manipulation and deceit, of a web of control that extended far beyond the Workshop.

Why here? I asked, watching him cradle the can like a precious relic.

He looked up at me, eyes clearer than they had been all night. This tree is a place of secrets. A place where things are hidden, buried deep. Just like us, Charles. We're buried in our own lies, our own masks. He opened the can again, displaying the poems and the documents. These are my real words, my real thoughts. Not the stuff they make me write. These are my truths, hidden from the world.

But why hide them? I pressed, feeling the weight of his despair.

Because the truth is dangerous, he whispered. It can destroy everything. If they knew what I really thought, they'd kill me. They'd kill us all.

Years later, I returned to the field outside of town. The cherry tree stood silent, a solitary figure in an ocean of grass. The night was thick with fog, the air cold and unfeeling. I dug at the base, the same spot where Carver had buried his secrets. Each shovelful felt like tearing open old wounds, unearthing dark whispers of the past. Finally, I found the ammo can, still there, still holding its cryptic contents. I pried it open, my hands trembling. Inside were Carver's poems, his true work, hidden from the world. They told a story of manipulation and deceit, of a web of control that extended well beyond the Workshop. Among the papers were stories attributed to Osiris Mandarin.

Back at the Workshop, the atmosphere grew increasingly tense. Huxley had become a shadow, lurking at the edges of my classes, his presence a constant reminder of unseen eyes and ears. I discovered later he had a student hide a tape recorder in his backpack during one of my lectures. That day, the discussion was on the role of the author in fiction. I ranted about the author being a capitalist myth, a construct to boost book sales. The Workshop is funded by the RAND Corporation. We are instruments of The Regime, our books no different from nuclear bombs in suitcases. The students sat in stunned silence, faces masks of confusion and fear. That's enough, Huxley said, his voice cold and authoritative. Leave the Workshop. His words were final, the door to my academic life slammed shut. He walked me to my office, his grip firm on my arm. This has been a long time coming, Charles. The scandal, the whispers, the tension. You think we didn't know about your little bar on South Clinton Street? You think we didn't know what you were scribbling? The Workshop, The Regime, they know everything. It's time for you to go.

Desperate and determined, I fled to East Berlin. The Wall loomed large, casting long shadows over our divided lives. I came in search of Osiris Mandarin. Berlin was a maze of contradictions. I encountered many who claimed to know Osiris, others who insisted he didn't exist, that he was a committee, like Homer. The search was maddening, each lead a thread that frayed into nothingness.

In the midst of my search, I met Elke, a typist at the Ministry of Culture. She was a true communist, her belief in the power of words unwavering. We married quickly, our union a blend of love and shared purpose. I began writing revolutionary stories for an underground magazine called Die Wahrheit. The magazine was run by a clandestine network of writers and activists, a crucial outlet for those who sought to speak the unspeakable.

Elke introduced me to the inner workings of the magazine. Hidden in the basement of an old bookstore, the editorial team worked tirelessly, their faces etched with determination and fear. They smuggled my writings across the Wall, passing them through a network of couriers who risked their lives for the cause. My stories, written under the name Osiris Mandarin, were like smoldering coals and sparks. They ignited the spirits of students and dissidents across Europe. In those turbulent years, my words rang out in fiery speeches in Paris, Budapest, and West Berlin. The horror of communism gripped me—the people were not free to be themselves; they feared being themselves. This realization fueled my obsession. I wrote feverishly, sending pages to magazines across the world. Revolutionaries ferried my words across the Wall, each passing fraught with danger.

One night, a courier named Tomas was caught. He was a young man, barely out of his teens, recklessly desperate for freedom. The Regime interrogated him brutally, and under duress, he confessed to being Osiris Mandarin. He was shot, and his death made the front page. Osiris Mandarin killed by Americans, shot trying to escape to East Berlin, the headlines screamed. The news hit me like a blow. Osiris Mandarin had become a symbol, a name that carried the weight of rebellion and resistance. Tomas's death was a reminder of the price we paid, the lives sacrificed for the truth.

As I sat in my cramped, dimly lit apartment in East Berlin, the air thick with despair and the stench of overused cooking oil. I smoked incessantly, each drag a desperate attempt to fill the emptiness. My thoughts turned to Carver, to the ammo can and the secrets it held. I used some of the material in my writings, weaving the threads of manipulation and control into my stories.

The paranoia grew. I saw shadows in every corner and felt eyes on me at all times. My work became darker and more urgent. Die Wahrheit published my most enduring pieces, stories that spread across Europe. My words became rallying cries, shouted in speeches by students in Prague, Warsaw, and Rome.

The Regime eventually caught up with me. They dragged me into a cold room with bare, unforgiving walls. My interrogator was a man of contradictions, cold yet erudite. We smoked and discussed Raskolnikov, our conversation a dance of shadows and philosophies. Identity and responsibility, he said, puffing out smoke like mushroom clouds. The Leviathan is mankind's only hope. Without it, the apocalypse is certain. His words were ominous, leaving an unsettling silence.

Finally, they took me to a wall. Elke stood beside me, her face pale but resolute. The Regime men raised their guns, and in that final moment, I felt a strange sense of clarity. My words, my identity, my life—only insignificant fragments in the grand tapestry of deception and control.

The shots rang out, piercing the cold, still air. We fell together, our bodies entwined, our secrets buried in the shadows of history.

27

LUCIA

I'VE ALWAYS FELT like a disappointment—to my mother, to society, and often, to myself. I am Lucia Bianchi, a sculptor living in Trastevere, a neighborhood in Rome where the past and present intertwine. Here, every cobblestone, every ivy-covered wall tells stories of history and defiance. Amidst the vibrant energy of artists and dreamers, I strive to free myself from the chains of my past.

My father died in the war, leaving my devoutly Catholic mother to raise me alone. Her faith became a fortress, both impenetrable and suffocating. She saw my art as an affront to God, a blasphemy I could never atone for. Her words, sharp as knives, cut deep. You are an abomination, Lucia, she would say. Your sculptures oppose the will of God.

Her criticisms bound me, but I found a way to break free in my mind. I created Osiris Mandarin, a pseudonym under which I wrote anti-Regime and political essays. To the outside world, Osiris was a voice of defiance against conformity. To me, Osiris was a way to reclaim my identity.

Trastevere was my haven, a bohemian enclave where artists found solace among like-minded souls. My studio on Via della Scala was a small, cluttered space where I molded clay and metal into expressions of freedom and identity. Around the corner on Vicolo del Bologna, Giovanni's Bookshop was a sanctuary for those who sought forbidden knowledge. Giovanni, a former partisan, had turned his shop into a hub for subversive literature. His dedication to literature was inspiring, shadowed by memories of war.

Piazza di Santa Maria was the heart of Trastevere, and Rosa's Café was its soul. Rosa, with her kind eyes, served coffee and pastries to the artists and intellectuals who frequented her café. She had lost her husband in the war and found comfort in listening to our stories. Enzo, the butcher on Vicolo del Bologna, was another fixture in the neighborhood. His gruff exterior hid a tender heart, and he often recited poetry while wrapping meat for his customers. His words were a surprising contrast to his rugged hands.

And then there was Marco. He worked as a waiter at a nearby trattoria. Marco was much younger than me, a fact that didn't escape the gossiping tongues of Trastevere. But Marco made me feel visible and beautiful, a gift I cherished in my fifty years of life. His presence was a balm to my wounded soul, a reminder that I was more than the sum of my mother's harsh words.

My life followed a rhythm, sculpting by day, writing by night. As Osiris Mandarin, I poured my fury into my writings, condemning the repressive ideologies of The Regime that demanded conformity. The Regime sought to erase individual identity, to replace it with a collective sameness that sickened me. My sculptures reflected this struggle—enormous heads bound in chains. I am not subtle.

One day, my fragile peace shattered during a public exhibit of my work. I had displayed my latest piece, a massive head bound in rusted chains, eyes hollow and pleading. The crowd murmured appreciatively, their admiration a fleeting balm. Then Father Paolo, a priest from the local parish, stepped forward. His face, lined with righteous indignation, contorted as he pointed at my sculpture.

This work is an abomination, he declared, his voice echoing through the gallery. It is opposed to the will of God. How dare you defile His creation with such monstrosities.

The words hit me like a blow, reigniting the old wounds my mother had left. The crowd fell silent, eyes shifting between me and the priest. My heart pounded in my chest, but I stood my ground, defiance burning in my veins.

This is my truth, Father, I replied steadily. These chains symbolize the oppression that binds us all. My work calls for freedom and individual identity. If that is a sin, then I embrace it fully.

The encounter left me shaken but resolute. That night, I retreated to my studio and wrote feverishly as Osiris Mandarin. My words were a scathing critique of both religious and political oppression, a declaration of war against The Regime that sought to silence me.

Days turned into weeks, and life in Trastevere continued.

Giovanni distributed banned books, Rosa's café buzzed with conversations, and Enzo's poetic recitations became a comforting routine. Marco and I found solace in each other's arms, his presence a constant reminder of beauty amidst the ruin.

One afternoon, Giovanni introduced me to a journalist named Robert. Giovanni spoke highly of Robert, saying he had a deep understanding of political and ideological struggles. Lucia, this is Robert, Giovanni said softly but firmly. He knew George Orwell during the Spanish Civil War. Robert, this is Lucia, the sculptor I've been telling you about.

Robert smiled, his eyes kind and thoughtful. It's a pleasure to meet you, Lucia. Giovanni has spoken highly of your work.

As we talked, I learned Robert had seen the horrors of fascism firsthand. He had been a journalist in Spain, where he met Orwell and witnessed the brutality of the Spanish Civil War. Robert claimed Orwell had been an Osiris Mandarin, a pseudonym for those who fought against oppressive regimes.

Our fight is not just against fascism or communism, Robert said steadily. It is against any ideology that seeks to erase individuality and impose conformity. Orwell understood this deeply, and so do you, Lucia. Your art is a powerful weapon in this fight.

Over time, Robert became my mentor. He helped me understand the history of political and ideological oppression, sharing stories of Orwell and his experiences. Through his guidance, I began to see the importance of individual liberty more clearly. Robert taught me how signs, symbols, and language shape thought and action, and how art can be a form of resistance.

One evening, as we sat in my studio discussing our work, Robert told me about a controversial poetry professor from Iowa named Charles Stone. Charles had been a rising star at the Iowa Writers' Workshop, known for his radical ideas and fierce independence. But his defiance had not gone unnoticed by The Regime.

Charles Stone was a brilliant mind, Robert said, lighting a cigarette and exhaling a cloud of smoke. He challenged the status quo, questioned everything. His poems on identity and resistance captivated many, but they also made him a target.

Robert explained how The Regime had orchestrated a scandal to discredit Charles, accusing him of submitting others' work as his own. The accusations were vicious, and the fallout was devastating. Charles was ostracized, his career in ruins. But he didn't disappear; he fled to East Berlin, becoming a ghost, a symbol of defiance.

Charles's story is a cautionary tale, Robert continued. But it's also a reminder of the power of resistance. He never stopped fighting, even when everything was taken from him. His work continues to inspire those who dare to speak out.

Robert's words lingered with me. I saw parallels between Charles's struggle and my own. The Regime's reach was long, and its grip was tight, but our voices could still pierce through the darkness.

Another evening, Robert shared stories of Raymond Carver, a writer who had worked for The Regime as part of their covert operation to influence American literature and culture. Carver's stories, seemingly mundane, were laced with subtle propaganda, designed to mold minds and manipulate emotions.

Raymond Carver's story shows how art can be weaponized, Robert said. The Regime uses every tool at its disposal to maintain control. We must be vigilant, always questioning the narratives we are fed.

As we continued our discussions, Robert's teachings illuminated the unseen battles we faced every day. He spoke of psychological guerrilla warfare, the necessity of reclaiming our minds as a form of resistance. The most dangerous prison, he remarked, is the one constructed within our own psyche. We must dismantle these mental chains to truly fight back.

Robert's insights into identity and resistance offered a new perspective, a focused lens through which to view our struggle. He proposed the idea of psychic insurgency, where the mind itself becomes a battleground for autonomy. Every thought, every dream that defies The Regime's narrative is an act of rebellion.

One day, I arrived at Robert's apartment to find it empty. There was no note, no sign of where he had gone. Only his notebooks and journals remained, filled with his thoughts and experiences, many of which contained references to Osiris Mandarin. As I read through Robert's writings, I felt a deep connection to his words. He had left behind a legacy of defiance, demonstrating the power of individual liberty. His stories of Orwell and the fight against fascism became a source of inspiration for me. I realized that Robert had been more than a mentor; he had been a guide, showing me the path to my own liberation.

One notebook in particular caught my eye. It was filled with references to Osiris Mandarin, suggesting the pseudonym was more than just a name—it was a mantle passed down through those who fought against oppression. I felt a surge of purpose, knowing that I was part of a larger struggle.

As I continued my work, I felt Robert's presence with me. His teachings, his stories, his unwavering belief in the power of art, all guided my hands as I molded the clay. My sculptures grew bolder, my writings fiercer. I knew that I was carrying on the legacy of Osiris Mandarin, a torch of defiance against the forces that sought to silence us.

In Trastevere, life continued. Giovanni's bookstore promoted dissident writers. Rosa's café remained a haven for artists and intellectuals, her tragic past reminding everyone of the strength found in community. Enzo's poetic recitations grew more impassioned, his words capturing the power of art. Marco, my beautiful yet simple Marco, stayed by my side, his presence a comforting constant. We loved each other in the quiet moments between my work and his shifts at the trattoria. He made me feel seen and cherished, a gift I held close to my heart.

But as days passed, the sense of urgency grew. Robert's disappearance left a void, and threats from The Regime became more palpable. Whispers about Dragan, an influential figure in the resistance movement now operating in Berlin, reached me. Giovanni had mentioned Dragan before, speaking of his crucial role in coordinating the fight against The Regime.

One evening, as I was locking up my studio, Giovanni approached me, his face etched with concern. Lucia, we need to talk, he said, glancing around nervously. Dragan is in Berlin, and he's been asking about you. He believes you can help with the resistance efforts there.

Berlin, I repeated, feeling a mix of fear and determination. The city where the fight against The Regime was fiercest, where Robert had said Charles Stone had fled. The pieces were falling into place.

Giovanni nodded. Yes, and with Robert gone, Dragan is the best person to help you understand the true meaning of Osiris Mandarin.

That night, as I lay in Marco's arms, my mind was a turbulent sea of thoughts. The decision to leave Rome and seek out Dragan in Berlin weighed heavily on me. But I knew it was the right choice. My work as Osiris Mandarin was far from complete, and the resistance needed every voice it could muster.

Marco sensed my restlessness. You have to go, don't you? he said softly, his eyes filled with understanding.

I nodded, tears welling up. Yes, I do. It's what I have to do.

Marco held me close. Then go. I'll be here when you get back. Just promise me you'll stay safe.

As dawn broke, I packed my bags, the promise of revolution heavy in the air. Giovanni handed me a train ticket and a letter of introduction to Dragan. Berlin awaited, a city draped in shadows and secrets. I was ready to uncover them, no matter the cost.

The streets of Trastevere were quiet as I left, the familiar sights and sounds fading behind me. I felt a renewed sense of purpose. My journey was far from over. The fight against The Regime was just beginning, and I would do whatever it took to see it through.

I boarded the train, my heart heavy with resolve. Berlin was calling, and I had to answer. Dragan awaited, and with him, the next chapter in the fight for freedom.

28

HANS BRECHT

THE SPARTAN IS DEAD. Hans Brecht is dead. They just don't know it yet.

The pistol pressed against my ribs, its weight a constant companion. The air outside The Kraken was tense, a reminder of the power games we all played. East Berlin was a city of shadows, and in this twilight, I was the hunter.

Amnon Mint was my prey. Word had reached me that he was slipping through the cracks, heading towards The Kraken—a tattoo parlor turned bar after Viktor's death. Once a den of resistance, now it was a watering hole for ideologues with more talk than action.

I stepped inside, the dim light casting long shadows on the faces of resistance members huddled around tables. They spoke in hushed tones, murmuring discontent and conspiracy. Weak. They were all weak. No leaders, no direction, just a collection of lost souls clinging to each other in the dark.

I found a seat in the corner, scanning the room. Press check. Slide back, round chambered. My 1911 was ready. Always ready. The name Hans Brecht felt foreign on my tongue, but it would serve its purpose tonight.

A man at the bar noticed my presence and asked who Brecht was, his voice cutting through the fog of conversations. Just a writer, I replied, lighting a cigarette. The smoke curled around my head, mingling with the scent of stale beer and unwashed bodies. Used to contribute to Osiris Mandarin.

That got their attention. Heads turned, eyes narrowed in suspicion and curiosity. The myth of Osiris Mandarin held a strange power here, a symbol of defiance and resistance.

As I nursed my drink, I observed. They were leaderless, directionless. Discussions turned to arguments, arguments to silence. They were playing at resistance, too afraid to take real action. Democracy, they called it. I called it chaos.

It wasn't long before I spotted Mint, slipping through the crowd like a ghost. His eyes met mine, and I saw a flicker of recognition. I nodded subtly, signaling him to follow me outside.

In the alley, the rain fell in a steady rhythm, masking our conversation. Mint was cautious, always looking over his shoulder. He asked if I wrote under Osiris Mandarin. A few pieces, I lied smoothly. Enough to know the resistance is falling apart. No leadership, no action.

Mint snorted, lighting his own cigarette. They're a bunch of paranoid fanatics, he said. Sitting around, talking. Doing nothing. It's pathetic.

I feigned agreement, comparing them to early Christians.

All faith, no backbone. They need someone to whip them into shape.

He eyed me critically. And you think you're the one to do it?

Maybe, I said with a shrug. But from what I've gathered, you know more about what's really going on. Rumor has it they're planning something big.

He took a deep drag, exhaling slowly. They are, but they're secretive. They don't trust anyone. Half of them think the other half are spies.

I leaned in, lowering my voice. What do you think?

Mint smirked, a cold, calculating expression. I think they're a bunch of terrorists. But I also think they might actually pull it off if they get their act together.

I played the sympathetic fool, nodding along. Maybe they need a push. Someone to steer them in the right direction.

Mint's eyes narrowed, and for a moment, I thought he might see through my facade. But then he relaxed, flicking his cigarette into the rain. Maybe you're right. But it's going to take more than words to make them move.

We walked back to The Kraken, the rain mingling with the dim light of streetlamps. I felt Heinrich Heinz Baumann's eyes on me before I saw him. He stood at the bar, his posture tense, his gaze cutting through the smoky haze. An old hand in the resistance, Baumann had seen too much and trusted too little.

He approached me, his eyes narrowing. You say you're Hans Brecht? A writer for Osiris Mandarin?

That's right, I said, maintaining my calm.

Heinrich leaned closer, his voice low and dangerous. I

don't trust you. Something about you doesn't sit right. Maybe you're just another spy for The Regime.

The room went quiet, tension thick in the air. I could feel the weight of eyes on us, the murmurs of the resistance members growing louder.

I understand your suspicion. In these times, trust is a rare commodity. But I assure you, I'm here to help. My voice was steady, even as my hand moved closer to my side, ready to draw if necessary.

Heinrich's eyes bore into mine, searching for a crack in my facade. What kind of help? Words don't mean much here.

Action, I said, leaning in, lowering my voice to a whisper. The resistance needs direction, leadership. We're wasting time talking when we should be acting.

Heinrich's hand twitched towards his coat pocket, and I knew he was ready to draw a weapon. You talk a lot for someone new here, he said, his voice a growl. Why should we trust you?

Because I want the same thing you do. A future where The Regime no longer controls our lives. I've seen what they do to people, and I won't stand by and let it happen anymore. My eyes locked on his, unwavering.

Heinrich studied me for a moment longer, then slowly nodded. But I'm watching you, Brecht. One wrong move, and you're done.

Understood. Let's make sure it doesn't come to that.

Heinrich walked away, but I could feel his eyes on me, still wary. I had planted the seeds of doubt in Mint and now in Heinrich. The game was becoming more complex, but I thrived in complexity.

I joined Mint at the bar again, signaling the bartender for water. Mint smirked, impressed with how I handled Baumann. He saw Baumann as a tough nut to crack, like an old friend from the academy who saw conspiracies in every shadow. Mint recalled how this friend, paranoid and distrustful, had accused the wrong person and ended up on the receiving end of a blade. Paranoia can be as deadly as a bullet.

Mint chuckled, noting Baumann's distrust. He mentioned how Baumann had seen too many friends turn traitor, making him question if it was the friends or the cause that was flawed. I noted it was the lack of strong leadership. People needed direction, a firm hand to guide them. Without it, they floundered, lost in their own doubts and fears.

Mint nodded thoughtfully, considering the resistance needed someone to make the tough decisions. He believed he could be that person, but knew they would never accept him. Too paranoid, too set in their ways. I suggested it was someone like us who needed to show them a new way, a way that actually worked.

Mint was exactly what I needed—a self-serving opportunist with no real allegiance. He could be manipulated, used to feed information back to The Regime. In this world of shadows, trust was a luxury few could afford. But deception? Deception was my weapon, and I wielded it well.

I noticed Heinrich still watching us, his eyes full of suspicion. Mint's disillusionment with the resistance was like a shadow clinging to him. He didn't care for their cause, only his own ambitions. The resistance was just a stepping stone for him. He was useful for now, but I wasn't tied to them. I saw Mint as a pawn in my game, a tool to gather information on Osiris Mandarin and feed it to The Regime.

In this world of shadows, only the cunning survived. And I intended to survive.

Mint finished his drink and stood up, looking at me with a glint in his eye. He said he was going to hear Dexter Jones play. The game was far from over.

29

FREE JAZZ

THE CLUB BUZZED WITH MURMURS, the clinking of glasses, and the rustle of newspapers. Headlines shouted about the Cold War, the Berlin Wall, and Kennedy's promises. In the shadows, whispers of underground movements and smuggled literature spoke of freedom. My fingers danced over the keys, twisting Beethoven's Moonlight Sonata into something rebellious. They didn't get it. They never would. The request for The Depths of My Sorrow felt like a slap in the face. I paused, took a drag from my cigarette, and spat out the words: shut up, motherfucker. The man nodded, but his eyes were filled with unmistakable hatred.

I played something dissonant and jarring. The audience listened, some captivated, others uncomfortable. A record executive watched with calculating eyes, already seeing profits. I ignored him, channeling my frustration into the keys. This wasn't about money. It was about breaking free. I wanted to jazz up the old masters—Beethoven, Bach, Mozart —breathing new life into their compositions.

After the set, I moved through the club, with offers of drinks constantly coming my way. Coffee was my refuge, a shield against the demons that claimed so many in this smoky world of shadows. Outside, the Berlin night was cold, the Wall looming as a specter of division.

The search for a studio in West Berlin had been futile. Every place felt wrong, sterile, devoid of the genuine authenticity I craved. Desperation led me to Johann, an old friend in East Berlin. His voice on the phone was a lifeline, a promise of something real. We agreed to meet at Checkpoint Charlie, the crossing a necessary step toward musical freedom.

Klaus drove me in his beat-up VW Beetle, the engine sputtering in protest. As we approached the checkpoint, the line was long, the tension palpable. Klaus's voice was a whisper of the past, reminiscing about times when the world seemed less defined, more fluid.

I used to have an apartment near the Wall, he said, lighting a cigarette. There was this woman, I think she was Russian, who lived in the building right across from me in the East. She'd play Shostakovich, Rachmaninoff, Prokofiev. But sometimes, just sometimes, she'd sprinkle in a little jazz —Bill Evans, Dave Brubeck. You had to be hip to catch it; she wove it into the classical stuff so seamlessly.

He took a deep drag, the smoke curling around him. I used to drink vodka and toast her while she played. She never knew. It felt like we had this secret connection through the music. I'd sit there, glass in hand, listening to her play, feeling like she was speaking directly to me.

He sighed, eyes distant. One day, the music stopped. I think they shot her. He giggled, the sound hollow in the cold air. Time seemed to slow down in that moment. He lit another cigarette. His words swam around slowly in the smoke until we reached the checkpoint.

An American soldier, a black guy, examined my papers. I recognized that grin. He'd seen me play back in Harlem, at Frank Jackson's club. I'd shut up Frank's loudmouth son, Larry, one night. Called him a motherfucker right there. Frank had my back, though. That was something.

I crossed into East Berlin. The buildings were grayer, the streets quieter. There was a sense of resilience, a quiet strength among the people.

Johann waited with his old Trabant, its engine stammering. The studio was a small, unassuming building tucked away on a narrow street. The exterior was worn, the paint peeling, the sign faded and barely legible. Inside, it was a different story.

The walls were lined with dark, weathered wood, absorbing the sound and giving the room a warm, intimate feel. The floor was scuffed and uneven, each creak underfoot adding to the atmosphere. Old, dusty instruments lay scattered around, each with its own history etched into the worn surfaces. The air was thick with the scent of cigarette smoke and aged leather, mingling with the faint aroma of coffee.

Microphones hung from the ceiling like relics from another era, their metal surfaces tarnished and dull. The recording equipment was a mix of the ancient and the modern, with vintage reel-to-reel tape machines sitting next to newer, sleeker devices. Cables snaked across the floor, creating a tangled web that seemed to pulse with the blood of jazz.

The lighting was dim, a single bare bulb casting long shadows across the room. It flickered occasionally, adding to the sense of time suspended, a place where the outside world ceased to exist. It was exactly what I needed—a space where I could strip away the pretenses and dive into the pure essence of the music.

Franz, the engineer, was an old man, no more than five feet tall, always smoking. His suit hung off him like a sack draped over a short pole. His sleeves were perpetually pushed up so he could use his hands. He never said much, just adjusted knobs and microphone locations with the precision of a surgeon. Some people said he used to be a detective, but he denied any connection to the police. He refused to talk politics, just stared anyone down who tried.

I had a vision. I wanted to take something sacred, like Beethoven's Moonlight Sonata, and make it groove. Turn it into modal jazz, mess with its structure, add drums and bass. The audience didn't want that. They thought it was distasteful. They just didn't get it yet. I'd show them.

Johann introduced me to Dragan, a man with wild eyes and an incessant need to talk about films and Jung. He claimed to have played with Mingus in Prague and now lived a transient life, sleeping on sofas and in parks. Dragan was full of it, but he could play. I needed a drummer, so I put up with his nonsense. If it weren't for the music, I would've popped him.

Call me Socrates, Dragan said with a manic grin, tapping a cigarette against his worn leather jacket. Music is a dialogue. Just like the collective unconscious. A symphony of archetypes playing out their roles.

Despite his quirks, we had no choice but to take him in. Dragan's drumming was unpredictable, a blend of jazz and madness that infused the music with a jagged, unpolished edge.

During a break in recording, Dragan leaned back in his chair and began to speak, his cigarette smoke curling around his words.

You know, Dexter, music and math are deeply connected, he said, eyes gleaming. Take Hilbert spaces. Infinite-dimensional spaces where every point is a possible state of the system. Think of the possibilities for music. Each note, each chord, expanding in infinite dimensions. It's like every time we play, we're exploring a different part of that space.

I told Dragan I'd pop him if he didn't shut up. I needed to think. The street performer's music, her words, had struck a chord deep within me. I needed to express the intensity and yearning I felt, but in a way that went beyond the notes I played.

The night before, I took a walk to clear my head. The streets of East Berlin were a maze of shadows and whispers. I found myself near the Wall, where a lone street performer played a melancholy melody on her violin. Her music was filled with an unspoken pain that sang to my own.

I stopped to listen, the notes filled with sorrow and defiance. She finished her piece and looked up, her eyes meeting mine.

Beautiful, I said softly, lighting a cigarette.

Merci, she said.

We stood in silence for a moment, the night paused. Then she began to play again, and I felt the words forming in my mind, the beginnings of a new poem.

That night, I sat in my small apartment. My wife, a schoolteacher and devout communist, was reading at the kitchen table. She knew I was in another place, that place I go sometimes. I'd been thinking about finding another way to express myself. Beyond music. I had some truths I wanted to tell.

The next day, I met with Pavel, an underground journalist whose eye twitched like he had a mosquito in it. He read my notebook and smoked a cigarette. Nodded his head as he read it, in time. I saw he got it.

This is good stuff, he said.

I leaned back, taking a drag from my cigarette. My writing needs to stay underground, away from The Regime.

Pavel reached into his bag and pulled out a worn copy of Shadows of Existence. He handed it to me, eyes serious. This book changed everything for me. The Regime fears words like these. Publish your work as Osiris Mandarin. Keep the flame alive.

Later that night, I sat in my apartment, the book heavy in my hands. The poems inside were unflinching, filled with a defiance that mirrored my own feelings. Osiris Mandarin was more than a name; it was a symbol of resistance, a way to fight back with words. The Regime feared this book, and now I understood why. It was a weapon, and I intended to use it.

We resumed recording, driven by an urgency that seemed to grow with each passing day. Dragan's drumming took on new intensity, as if he was channeling the frustrations and fears we all felt. Franz, always smoking and adjusting knobs, maintained his stoic silence, his eyes flickering with some unspoken wisdom.

One afternoon, there was a knock at the studio door. It opened to reveal a tall, thin man with wire-rimmed glasses and an air of conviction. Franz barely glanced up, but I saw a flicker of recognition in his eyes.

The man was Becker from the Ministry of State Security. His presence was like a cold wind sweeping through the room, chilling the air, making the smoke from my cigarette hang heavy, unmoving. He carried with him the weight of authority, a subtle menace that spoke volumes without uttering a single word.

Becker took a seat, the chair creaking under his lean frame. He exhaled slowly, the smoke from his cigarette curling upwards, merging with the haze already present. His eyes never left mine, studying, evaluating. There was something inherently subversive about jazz, he conveyed, something dangerous in its improvisation and freedom. It was a rebellion against constraints, an expression of unpredictability within structure.

I nodded cautiously. It was about expression. Giving voice to ineffable feelings.

Becker seemed to understand this, but his understanding was tainted by the need for control. Even in the most spontaneous moments, there must be structure, he seemed to say. Improvisation needed a foundation. Otherwise, it was just noise.

He looked around the studio with casual interest, noting

the worn instruments and vintage equipment. His gaze settled back on me, a silent question hanging in the air: what did I hope to achieve with my music? What drove me? I chose my words carefully, explaining that I wanted to express the human experience—the struggles, the joys. Music was a way to communicate when words failed.

Becker's nod was slow, thoughtful. A noble goal, but in this city, in this climate, everything had a consequence. Music, especially jazz, could inspire thoughts, actions, rebellion. The subtext was clear: even my art was not beyond the reach of the Regime's scrutiny.

Dragan, always eager to share his thoughts, interjected that jazz was about freedom.

Shut up, motherfucker, I said coldly, shooting him a glare.

Becker's eyes flickered with amusement, recognizing the tension within our group. It was a subtle reminder caution was necessary, that the walls had ears, that even here, in this sanctum of creativity, we were never truly free.

We kept recording, each session more intense than the last. Franz, always silent, always smoking, adjusted the mics and knobs with a precision that bordered on obsessive. I found myself writing more and more, the words flowing as if from some deep well within me.

One night, as we took a break from recording, Dragan leaned in, his eyes gleaming with excitement. I've been reading Brecht, he said. His ideas on epic theatre, the way he breaks the fourth wall, makes the audience think rather than feel. It's revolutionary.

I smirked. You think everything's revolutionary, Dragan.

Dragan's grin widened. Because everything is. Everything can be.

The tension reached its peak as the Regime's surveillance intensified. My paranoia grew, each shadow and whisper adding to my fear. The inevitable arrest came one cold, gray morning. My wife, her mother, and I were taken from our home, the air thick with the stench of fear and inevitability.

We were led to an interrogation room, the atmosphere heavy with dread. Becker entered, his expression inscrutable. He adjusted his glasses, then lit a cigarette, exhaling slowly as he regarded us.

He began talking about jazz, about structure within improvisation. Said my poetry was like my music. Beautiful, but dangerous in its defiance.

I tried to meet his gaze, my mind racing. I wrote about freedom. About the human spirit. That wasn't a crime. Becker's smile was thin, almost pitying. In this world, freedom could be the most dangerous idea of all. A threat to order. To stability. I had inspired many, but inspiration could lead to rebellion.

As he spoke, the door creaked open and Franz entered, his eyes avoiding mine. He handed Becker a folder, then left without a word. My stomach sank as I realized the truth. Franz had been informing on me, on all of us.

Becker's gaze shifted to the side, a slight smirk playing on his lips. You know, Dexter, you really should have played The Depths of My Sorrow. Sometimes, compliance is survival.

As the truck rattled down the narrow streets, my wife leaned into me, her warmth a stark contrast to the cold, metal interior. Her mother clutched a faded photo, her lips moving in silent prayer. I watched as familiar landmarks faded into the distance, each one a relic of lost possibilities.

We were led to a brick wall, the backdrop to our final moments. The officers from the Regime were cold and indifferent, their eyes devoid of empathy. Becker stood to the side, watching silently.

He leaned closer, voice a whisper of steel. The Osiris Mandarins are being erased. One by one. You thought you could hide behind that name. We know everything, Dexter. Finn O'Malley's entire plan is in our hands now.

I looked at him, baffled. Who the hell is Finn O'Malley?

His smirk was icy. Ignorance won't save you now, he said.

Shut up, motherfucker.

Becker nodded. A staccato of shots. I'll never get to finish my record.

30

JOHNY

THE TRAILER PARK IS A GRAVEYARD, each mobile home a tombstone marking lives that went nowhere. I sit on my steps as the Texas sun casts long shadows across the cracked earth. The world is silent, except for a passing car and a distant barking dog. I light a Camel, watching the smoke curl into the dry air.

Tommy drives by in his rusted Ford F-100, the radio blaring conspiracy theories. He lives two trailers down, a redneck with his old Ford on cinder blocks. He did time for boosting cars and has a kid named Billy he never sees. The radio's got him brainwashed; he has no idea what the truth is.

I take a swig of Jack Daniels, admiring its label as a work of underappreciated art, better than most museum pieces. The burn distracts me from my thoughts. The trailer park is the only place I feel safe, even though I'm haunted by memo-

ries of good men who did bad things. Men who now have
proper graves, nothing like this shithole.

Every morning, I drive to a clearing in the woods to train.
My Browning Hi-Power is concealed under my shirt. I press-
check it every time. I killed six men in Korea with it. To most,
I'm the Man with No Name. Training keeps me sharp. I
imagine an old Western showdown: draw, fire, holster. Quick,
precise, final.

I get into my truck, the engine coughing to life. My hand
instinctively reaches for the pistol. I press-check it, feeling its
familiar weight and balance. My gut tells me something's off.
It's not just Tommy's paranoia rubbing off on me. It's the
pattern, the rhythm of things shifting. You can feel it now.

On the way back, I stop at the gas station to buy cigarettes. The clerk, a lanky kid with acne scars, barely glances
up. I notice the headlines on the newspapers by the
counter; student protests are happening everywhere. The
kid looks puzzled and asks if I think the Russians will come
here. He seems confused and lost. I pause, surprised by the
question. Russians? Kid, this place isn't important enough
for them. Little does he know how close to the truth he
might be.

Outside, Tommy struggles with the hood of his Ford. The
truck won't start. I help him out. The distributor cap is loose,
a common problem with these models. I tighten the cap, and
the engine roars to life. He nods gratefully and mentions
seeing a white van outside my trailer last night, showing a lot
of interest in my place. This is news to me. I haven't done
anything. He warns that trouble might be sniffing around,
then drives off.

I smoke a cigarette at the gas pump before heading back to the trailer park.

The night settles in, the air thick with anticipation. Mullet starts barking, not his usual bark—something more urgent. My hand instinctively reaches for the Browning. It's 3 AM. Can't be the mailman. I step outside, the cool night air wrapping around me. I see the white van parked at the edge of the trailer park. Three men are smoking and chatting, too casual for this hour. My training kicks in. I switch into the Man with No Name. Violence of action. I rush. Before they can reach for their guns, my barrel is centered on the one with the cowboy hat.

He raises his hands, speaks with a thick Russian accent. Is good, comrade. We go now.

They back away, get into the van, and drive off without another word. I stand there, gun still raised, until their tail-lights disappear into the darkness. My past has found me. I feel like the outlaw who just cleared out the saloon.

Back inside, I pour another drink, light another Camel. Townes Van Zandt's voice drifts softly from the old record player. The whiskey burns a familiar path down my throat, the smoke curls around me, and I think about the shadows that never quite leave you.

Sleep comes reluctantly. I drift in and out, haunted by visions of the past and the future colliding. When I finally wake, the light of dawn is filtering through the blinds, casting long, thin shadows across the room.

I hear the sound of rustling paper and my eyes snap open. Marek is sitting in my worn-out armchair, my Browning resting casually on his knee. In his hands, he's flipping through my notebook, the one filled with poems and stories signed Osiris Mandarin. He looks up, asks if I've been writing much.

The secret's out. He closes the notebook, unreadable expression. Many in the resistance read your work. It gives them hope, a reason to fight. Does Finn know you're Osiris Mandarin?

No one knows, I reply.

Marek didn't think poetry was much of a weapon. I tell him it is when it's the truth. He calls me the fighter and the poet, says Berlin needs Osiris Mandarin. Berlin? I ask. He tells me Finn O'Malley's there and things are heating up. Every hand we can get, every mind. Words, skills—they're both weapons now.

I stand up, the weight of Marek's news settling over me. Finn's back in Berlin? Marek hands me my Browning, his eyes grave. We need you both. Berlin's about to go up in flames, like that Regime building Finn took down for Mary. But much, much bigger.

Lucia did it. She acquired the suitcase from Babushka Anya.

31

THE COPERNICAN SHIFT

THE BERLIN safe house serves as our command center. Behind Dragan, Jonathan's chalkboard is covered with calculations and diagrams. Dragan paces, his gaze intense, hair long and unruly like Pyotr Verkhovensky. He stops and turns to us, eyes alight with fervor. He picks up his camera and adjusts the lens. This isn't an attack. It's an ideological discontinuity, he says.

He pauses, scanning our faces. We've been making small adjustments for too long, adding little Ptolemaic epicycles. No more. We need a Copernican shift. We'll put the sun at the center of The Regime. This is our Dr. Strangelove moment, cowboys.

He turns to the chalkboard, where Jonathan's calculations detail the blast radius and impact zones of our plan. This exactness, he says almost reverently, is our weapon. Jonathan's minimax strategy ensures the detonation minimizes collateral damage while maximizing Regime losses.

The world must see we are not mindless rebels but method-ical tacticians. He lifts his camera. This documentation is our testimony. Our narrative.

The haunting notes of Moonlight Sonata from Dexter Jones' record fill the room, underscoring Dragan's words. The music reminds us of what we fight for—a world where art and beauty exist without fear.

I move to the table, tracing the lines on the blueprints. Every detail has been considered, every guard shift, every entry point, carefully planned. We cannot afford mistakes.

Jonathan finishes his calculations. Timing is crucial. We'll have a window of exactly three minutes to get in, leave the package, and get out. Any deviation risks failure.

In the corner, Jonas sits quietly, a reminder of our intel-lectual battles. Betrayed by The Regime, his ideas stolen and twisted, he embodies the struggle for creative freedom.

Hans Brecht stands apart, seemingly absorbed in the plans but contributing little. There's something off about him. His demeanor, too calm. The way his eyes scan the room, probing. He's been with us for months, yet remains a mystery.

I light a cigarette, the smoke curling around me. Maureen and Mary deserved better than this. Tonight is for them. For everyone who has suffered. We make the final preparations in silence. The haunting notes of Moonlight Sonata continue to play.

In the corner, Johny sits, seemingly disinterested, methodically cleaning his pistol. His eyes, though, never leave Brecht. They follow his every move, every gesture, with a hawk-like intensity. He knows something about Brecht the rest of us don't.

We file out of the safe house, slipping into the night like shadows. The streets of Berlin are quiet, the oppressive presence of The Regime hanging heavy in the air. We navigate the underground tunnels with practiced ease, every step bringing us closer to our target.

At the final checkpoint, I turn to my team. Their faces are illuminated by the dim glow of our flashlights. This is it. No turning back now.

I take a deep breath, the haunting notes of Moonlight Sonata playing in my mind. I am going to put the sun inside this suitcase in the heart of The Regime. Maybe I will burn down the whole goddamn world.

For millennia, man remained what he was for Aristotle: a living animal with the additional capacity for a political existence; modern man is an animal whose politics places his existence as a living being in question.

— MICHEL FOUCAULT

ABOUT THE AUTHOR

Neil Bearden is Osiris Mandarin.

BOOK TWO

In the dim alleys of resistance, Book Two further explores secret whispers and ideological struggles. Characters navigate a broken landscape, manipulated like puppets by oppressive regimes. Words act as chains and keys, revealing freedom and confinement. The search for truth becomes a journey through ideological fog and shadows.

Osiris Mandarin Press

Made in the USA
Columbia, SC
17 April 2025